Big
Dildo
Night

POSSESS ME SLOWLY
The Shattered Series

JOYA RYAN

This is an original publication of Bear and Gunner Publishing, LLC.

Copyright © 2013 by Joya Ryan
ISBN-13: 978-1494927233
ISBN-10: 1494927233
Printed in the United States of America.
www.JoyaRyan.com

dedication

To YOU—My Reader.

It's is because of you that this book even exists. Your encouragement is the reason I wrote this story. I hope you enjoy it and thank you so much for all your support and standing by me!

You are AMAZING!

ACKNOWLEDGMENTS

Thank you to the E-book Formatting Fairies for your amazing editing job! Thank you Jill for just...everything. You rock so much and are a wonderful friend and killer agent! Thank you to Jenn LeBlanc and Viola Estrella, as always, the cover is incredible! And finally, thank you to my friends and family for your continued support!

TABLE OF CONTENTS

1

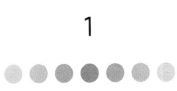

"I'm going to be an hour late."

I pressed the phone to my ear and listened to the one and only bartender tonight explain why he wouldn't be in on time. It was eleven in the evening, I was officially off work and had a two-day weekend to look forward to. Almost.

"I'll cover for you until you get here, Hector."

"Thanks Megan, you're the best."

Hanging up the phone, I straightened my white blouse and black skirt. Going from assistant manager to bartender at the Strauss Hotel in one night wouldn't be so bad if my day wasn't already a giant crap sandwich.

"It's just an hour," I mumbled to myself and grabbed my purse.

It wasn't like I had much of a life outside of work anyway. Even though there were over one hundred Strauss luxury hotels littered across the globe, the only location that had an open position with room for fast promotion was in Manhattan—and the position paid well. But leaving my family and friends back home in Chicago for the lonely city of New York had been an adjustment.

A few weeks ago, my best friend Kate's soon-to-be sister-in-law came to stay with me. Emma Wade and I had become close since Adam and Kate got together. She was looking to get out of

Chicago and I offered her my spare bedroom. Though she never told me details, her situation seemed urgent. I could understand that. We were friends, but we had a silent understanding that our reasons for fleeing to New York were our own.

But tonight she had plans, which meant another evening in an empty apartment.

Stretching my neck, I walked through the impressive lobby but couldn't seem to shed the invisible weight crashing down on my shoulders—probably because it was over six months of stupid mistakes that affected not only myself, but my parents as well.

My heels clicked on the shiny marble floors as I wound down the corridor and into the bar. The low lighting and slight smell of vanilla and bourbon was almost soothing. The Strauss Hotel Bar was a sleek, modern take on the rustic and rugged. Glossy cherry tabletops reflected tiny beams from the single candles atop them. If you didn't know better, you could mistake the surroundings for a high-end restaurant in Aspen.

Thank God it wasn't busy tonight. Only a couple of scattered patrons occupied the corner tables.

"Hi Megan," Shari said. Her short black bob bounced as she walked around the bar, untying her apron. "Where's Hector?"

"He's running a bit late so I'm covering."

Shari froze, hands on her apron. "Are you sure? I could stay."

"No, you've been here since the lunch shift."

Shari stepped closer and lowered her voice. "Yeah, but by the looks of it, you've been crying on and off all day."

A sharp breath stuck in my throat. Damn it. Running my fingertips under my eyes I took a deep breath. My father had been showing heavy signs of dementia right after I left for New York and it was getting worse. Quickly. That was the latest information I could decipher from my mother's voicemails and texts today. I would have gone home to help my mother take care of him, but since neither of them were working I needed my job so I could help support them.

"Is it your dad?"

"Yeah, he went to a specialist this morning and I have been waiting to hear back from my mom all day." It wasn't a lie. But it wasn't the whole truth.

"How is he doing?"

"Not good. He forgot who I was when I called yesterday. Called me Fresca." A small laugh escaped. Even to my own ears it sounded raw and wounded. "Fresca was my dog when I was eight."

Shari rested a hand on my arm and just the small contact made my chest tighten. "Megan, I am so sorry."

"Yeah, me too. I took this job so I could help with his bills, but now I feel I am too far away to really help. I don't know what to do."

"You know I'm here if you need me, right?"

I nodded and let myself take a deep breath. It was the only way to keep from crying. Sometimes it just felt as though everything was spinning out of control and that the weight I carried every day would eventually pull me under.

"Seriously, is there anything I can do?"

Shari had been working at The Strauss Hotel Bar for three years and was the only friend I had managed to make. She was a single mom who tended bar at night so that she could be home with her daughter during the day. And she knew all about my dad's problems—well, his health problems. No one knew about the *other* problems. Not even my best friend back home.

"Yes, go home to your beautiful daughter. Working will help keep my mind busy."

"If you're sure," she said, hesitating.

"I'm sure." I was more than sure. The only thing I wanted to do right then was just get lost, pretend that I was some bartender without a care in the world.

"Okay, well everyone is taken care of and it's been pretty slow. If you change your mind, just give me a call," she said, dropping her apron behind the bar and giving me a hug.

"I won't." My cell phone buzzed and I pulled it from my purse. "But thanks. Kiss Sydney for me."

Shari smiled and I headed behind the bar while reading the text from my mother:

Sorry I missed your call today, honey. Dr. Forman agreed to do a conference call tomorrow at one o'clock to discuss Dad. Love you.

I closed my eyes and willed myself to hold it together. If Dr. Forman wanted to talk, then things must have gotten exponentially worse. And I was stuck here, eight hundred miles away from where I was needed most.

After my longtime boyfriend Brian cheated on me with my best friend's aunt, who had fake boobs and very real money, I thought I had hit a low point. But when my boss tried to kissed me, only to then fire me, things rapidly spiraled out of control.

My ex-boss, Tim St. Roy, was charged with embezzling several million dollars from high-end clients in a real-estate scam. Tim was tried and convicted, his greed costing him ten years in a minimum-security prison. It cost my parents everything. The stolen funds were never recovered—and neither would my parents, since my advice to diversify and take a risk left them penniless.

I had turned their stable life into chaos. And now, my mother was too old for most available jobs and with no retirement, no way to pay for my dad's increasing medical expenses, and a second mortgage on the house, we were one bad month away from foreclosure.

Texting my mom that I would be on the call, I put my cell back in my purse and stepped behind the bar. One customer had already left and no one was at the counter. Maybe I could avoid actually waiting on someone until Hector got here. Then I could go home to my shoebox apartment and wallow in the most recent news—news that had me crying in the employee bathroom.

Brian and Grace had eloped.

My best friend Kate had called earlier, wanting to tell me before someone else did. My throat struggled to swallow the news and I seriously considered pouring myself a drink. I didn't care about Brian anymore, it was just the final blow after an already tough several months.

Skating my fingertips along my collar bone, I checked for some kind of physical sign of wear and tear. All the nasty things life dished out and built up had to go somewhere, right? Any day now I suspected I'd find a growth or a tumor.

"Rough night?"

My gaze snapped up and saw a very handsome, very imposing man sitting on the other side of the bar.

His chiseled jaw was lined with day-old scruff and his thick choc-olate hair was a little longer and slightly unruly. At one point it must have been perfectly combed, but judging by exhaustion in his dazzling green eyes, I guessed it had been a long day for Mr. Suit and Tie.

I batted my lashes to keep the tear that had been sneaking up on me at bay. "I'm fine, thank you. What can I get for you?"

He looked me over for a long moment, as if determining if I was telling the truth—which I wasn't.

"Gentleman Jack on the rocks. Although from the looks of things maybe I should be offering you a drink." His deep voice rolled over me more smoothly than the liquor he ordered, and the sound spread chills over my skin. Heat was licking on its heels leaving my body confused and achy.

"Man problems?" he asked.

I started pouring the drink. "Yes, but the particular man in question is now somebody else's problem." I forced a smile. "And even though I'd love to take you up on that drink, it's against corporate policy."

"And I take it you are one of those good girls who always follows the rules?"

When he put it that way I sounded so boring. No wonder Brian left me for another woman. "Unfortunately, yes."

He nodded. "A bartender with morals. Interesting."

The way he said interesting, his intense eyes running the length of me, made me feel anything but boring or good. It made me feel like doing something dangerous.

"Who hired you to tend bar?" Suit and Tie asked. His tone held more than a slight edge of disbelief.

I set his drink down in front of him, maybe a bit harder than I should have. "Excuse me?"

His gaze slid over me. That one heated look was apparently all the explanation I was getting. Too bad that *one look* also made those stupid goose bumps come back.

"I am just covering at the moment." He nodded, those green eyes strolling up and down my body once more as if he had the right to do so.

"You must be new," he rasped and took a long swallow of his drink. "I would have remembered seeing you."

"I've worked here six months now. You stay here often, Mr. …?"

He grinned and took another drink. "Preston. And yes, I travel a lot and stay here often."

"Well, pleasure to have you back." I gave my best "hospitality is our specialty" smile and tried to ignore the buzzing beneath my skin. The man was intimidating and starkly beautiful. His body was hard, like his unnerving eyes, but something about his presence was soothing. This was a man who was in control of his world and knew what he wanted. Power and confidence radiated from him but there was a relaxed essence surrounding him. The way his white collared shirt was rolled up at the sleeves, exposing his tan, strong forearms and Rolex—

Shit! He was not only a regular of the Strauss Hotel but one of "those." Between his demeanor and obvious money, he must be the kind of VIPer my whole team prepped for. I didn't remembered seeing a Mr. Preston on the check-in docket today, but between the chaos of being understaffed, my growing worry over my parents, and feeling nauseated about Brian and Grace eloping, I hadn't been on my A-game in terms of paying attention to details.

"What's your name?" He smiled over the edge of his glass and a whole different feeling fluttered in my stomach.

"Megan!" Hector called from across the room. He hustled over to me. "Thanks so much, I owe you."

"It's no problem." I turned my attention back to the man at the bar. "Nice meeting you."

I grabbed my purse from behind the counter just as the customer in the corner booth raised his empty glass in the air.

"I'll get that," Hector said, and went over to the guest. I stepped around the bar and tried not to look at Suit and Tie when I passed him.

"Aren't you going to help me with my bags?" he asked.

Now, I had to look at him. Mistake. There was a hunger in those brilliant greens that was hard to ignore. And I was too mentally exhausted to care that my long neglected body responded in every way.

"Excuse me?"

"You work here, don't you? Aren't you going to help me with my bags?" He pulled out his wallet and set money on the counter. I looked at the empty stool on each side of him.

"You don't have any bags."

He picked up his briefcase that rested near his feet and held it out to me.

"Are you serious?"

"Yes. You wouldn't want me to complain to management about your lack of hospitality."

"I am management."

"Then all the reason you should know better." A smile sliced across his face more shocking than the color of his eyes. Good lord, no man had a right to look this good.

He didn't let me respond, simply handed me his briefcase and placed his hand on the small of my back, instantly guiding me out of the bar. I really hated my body in that moment. Just the warmth from his palm, resting possessively low on the small of my back, sent shivers racing and thoughts about what his touch would feel like skin on skin. Thankfully, the elevators were close. He hit the penthouse button, a floor that was reserved for Strauss family members or the very highest esteemed guests. Again, I mentally hit myself for not being ready for this man's arrival.

"I didn't see you down on our log, Mr. Preston."

"I'm a day early."

My brain struggled to mentally go through the check-in list for tomorrow but unfortunately, I had forgotten to look at it before hustling to cover the bar tonight.

"Don't worry. I won't put it on the comment card that you don't know who I am or are unprepared for me."

"We're prepared!" I said a bit quicker than I meant just as the doors dinged open to the penthouse floor. He extended his arm, offering me to exit first. I did and took a left down the hall. A single door was at each end of the wing. The layout was massive. The penthouse had a separate office on the other side of the hall with its own outside door.

When I reached the entrance to the penthouse I was almost shaking. Today was a bust. I was upset, wired and now thanks to this elegant domineering stranger, horny.

"Well, have a pleasant evening, sir."

He grinned and took the key from his inside coat pocket and unlocked the door. He propped it open just enough to put his Italian leather-covered foot in the jamb, keeping it barely ajar.

"That was my hope," he said and his eyes shot to mine.

I stood there, clutching his briefcase, my heart banging out of my chest. He reached out and trailed his fingers down my arm, stopping at the death grip I had on the handle.

"Thank you for your service." The way he said those words were dark, yet had a playful undertone.

"You're welcome and if there is anything else you need don't hesitate to call."

He smiled and it sent my heart racing. "I don't have your number."

"I meant the front desk, sir."

"I know what you meant," he stepped closer, "And you know what I meant. Tell me, is it exhausting?"

"What?"

"Following all those rules?"

I couldn't think. Couldn't process what was happening. It was like some pheromone seeped from him and was rendering me totally complacent. I was actually considering what proposition lay in his eyes.

The way he looked at me. All of me. Like I was standing in front of him naked without shedding a stitch of clothing. My body hummed in such a traitorous way that my pulse pinched the tips of my breasts like sharp snapping fingers.

I let go of the briefcase and he took it. He squared his shoulders and all that masculine heat wrapped around me like a predator examining its target. It was obvious this man exerted power and got what he wanted. Only problem was, I was in his sights and had no idea how to react.

"I-I must be going, Mr. Preston."

"But you're not." He stepped closer, his breath fanning over my forehead, cornering me. I was considered tall for a woman. In heels I pushed five-ten, yet he was still a good four inches taller.

Somehow, he maneuvered me into the doorway, one foot inside the room, one still in the hall. I didn't know which way to step. The jamb of the entry pressed between my shoulder blades and my front was completely covered by a tower of muscle and spicy smelling yumminess.

Part of me wanted to run, but the practical part of my brain had shut down a while ago. I hadn't been this close to someone in a while. My entire being craved this man. Was begging for this nearness. I tried to look at the ceiling and break the spell Preston had over me, but two emerald beacons once again snared my attention.

My brain might be shot, but I knew this wasn't a good idea.

"I'm sorry. This is unprofessional. You're a guest and I'm an employee of the hotel." Even when I attempted to reprimand myself it didn't sound convincing.

"You're not on the clock," he whispered and traced a finger along my hairline from my temple to my ear. "Right now, you're just a woman. I'm just a man. No rules. No expectations. Just pleasure and escape."

A small moan escaped my mouth before I could stop it. I wanted to be swallowed up by everything he was offering. To let go. For one night give in to something good. Something intense. Forget that life was spinning around me and, for one night, pretend to exist in the moment. And judging by the fire in his eyes and the bulge pressing against my belly, *intense* would just be the beginning.

"You're just passing through, right?" It was the only thing I could think to say because his mouth crept dangerously close to mine.

"That a problem?"

"No," I whispered. It was actually better that way.

He tossed the briefcase into the room and it slammed onto the floor. In one fluid motion, his hands were on me. One cupping my hip and the other my face. He yanked me into his hard body and kissed me hard. Sliding his tongue between my lips, he drew in one strong taste, drinking down every piece of hesitation I had. Inhibitions vanished. One amazing kiss left me dazed and oh so willing.

"You never told me your name," he said and bit my bottom lip.

"Y-you heard it…"

"I want *you* to tell me."

"Megan," I whispered.

He gave a curt nod, as if that was all he needed. Which worked for me. The more details, the bigger the mess. Right now I reveled in the better part of my brain turning off and letting my body take over. I wanted to forget. Forget about a cheating boyfriend that broke my heart. The boss that stole my family's money. Forget that my father, the one man who had never let me down, was suffering from his own kind of forgetting—and it was starting with me.

My eyelids felt like they were lined with recently welded steel. I didn't want to be in my thoughts. I didn't want to be alone with them anymore. Tonight…it just felt like too much to bear. And staring down a sculpted build of masculine strength, it was the first time in a long time *forgetting* was actually possible.

He studied my face for a moment, as if he sensed a slight shift in my mood. I gripped the back of his neck and pulled him down.

"Please, Preston. Just kiss me."

The last six months of my life was disappeared with the barest of touches and his lips. Everything fell away, and that was exactly what I had wanted. This moment. Just him.

He slanted his mouth over mine. His large palm was still cupping my face and he pushed his thumb on my chin, opening my mouth wider. Delving his tongue inside, he took a deeper draw from my mouth like he was gulping down his last breath of air.

I'd never felt more consumed and we hadn't even gone past kissing. He didn't rush. Every lash of his skilled tongue was deliberate. Passionate. Long, hard strokes of his masterful mouth sent shivers to every part of my body.

I gently cupped his face in my palms, tracing my fingertips down his chin with slight pressure. I wanted to feel him. Feel his jaw work as he devoured me. The soft scratch of day-old stubble abraded my palms. He smelled, felt—kissed—like a man. So strong and controlled, like a well-oiled machine drawing every last ounce of willpower from me.

He pulled back just enough to look into my eyes. A frown split his dark brows. Had I done something wrong? I gently pulled my hands away.

"Don't," he grated. The words were sharp and cut through all the layers of misery I'd been carrying around. He gripped my wrists and guided my hands back to his face. "Don't take your hands from me. Understand?"

I nodded. It was an obvious order, but for the briefest of moments, I caught a glimpse of vulnerability behind the hardness of his eyes. His mouth was back on mine and he didn't slow down. His seeking tongue unleashed another dose of intensity and my whole body melted for him.

He pulled the hem of my tight skirt up a couple inches, allowing my legs freedom to bend and move better. Grabbing my ass, he hoisted me up. I instantly wrapped my legs around his hips and my arms around his neck. He gently bit the column of my throat as he maneuvered me into the penthouse. I heard the door shut behind us. He didn't stop, instead heading toward the bedroom.

I had no time to take in the surroundings. Dim light, the smell of fresh clean linen and then soft cotton. A mattress hit my back. He made quick work of his shirt, threw it off, and stood at the end of the bed. My breath caught when I tried desperately to inhale. But the sinful man staring me down was making a simple intake of oxygen difficult.

My God, he was gorgeous. Broad shoulders, thick, firm muscles that spread across his chest and down his torso. His abs were cut and coiled so tightly they resembled welded bronze.

Those haunting green eyes beamed against the soft light, never leaving mine as he took off my left stiletto, then the right. Sliding his hands up my shins, I stifled a moan at the warmth of his touch. His roughened palms scratched against my silk stockings. I felt so small. He could close his whole hand around my calf and probably touch thumb to finger.

He continued his slow assault up my body until he came to my skirt. He unclasped it and peeled it down my legs and off, leaving me in my white lace thong.

"Unbutton your top," he commanded.

I did. I opened each button, noting how my fingers were trembling with anticipation and nervousness. I'd never had a one-night stand before, never considered myself the kind of girl to have one, but nothing would have made me leave his bed—this moment.

I opened the fabric, baring my pale lacy bra that matched my panties.

He looked at me for a long moment, as if examining the entire length of my frame.

"White," he rasped. "Such an innocent color."

I glanced down my body. My stockings were nude but everything else was white. I'd never considered the "innocent" aspect before.

"You're a lovely woman, Megan." His voice was raw and heated but the words hit a chilly chord. It was a polite gesture, a baseline compliment designed to flatter yet maintain a distance, but I wanted to hear the words he was obviously holding back.

The words that accompanied the growl that vibrated from him when he kissed me.

I didn't want to hold back tonight. I didn't want to give in to responsibility and torturous thoughts. I wanted intensity. Unguarded words and actions. To hear what kind of words matched the man with a dominant stance and sexy stare.

"A lovely woman?" I asked and positioned myself on my knees. With my white shirt hanging open and decked out in matching lingerie, my goal was to project more sex appeal than "lovely."

Something that sounded like a low groan broke from his chest. I crawled toward him, confidence coursing through me. His eyes smoldered and I knew he was on the brink just like I was.

"Do you like 'lovely' girls, Suit?"

Crawl.

His hands fisted at his side and his gaze trailed from my face, to my breasts, then back up again. He didn't answer so I pushed with, "Maybe nice girls?"

Crawl.

"And if I do?"

I pushed to my knees again at the end of the bed. "Then I'm sure to disappoint you." Kneeling on the bed with him standing before me, I was eye level with his impressive chest.

"You look like a nice girl, Megan."

I had spent twenty-three years being nice and all it had gotten me was trouble. Nice was easy to walk all over, lie to and shatter. I was done with nice.

I gripped his belt and unfastened it. "Not tonight."

I couldn't be. The moment I started thinking was the moment reality weaseled its way back into my mind. No reality. No soft, sweetness. No *nice*.

His eyes remained on mine. A silent challenge to see how far I'd go. I unbuttoned his fly and reached into his boxer-briefs.

The man was endowed. Not bothering to take his pants completely off—because that would mean I'd have to give up what I was currently holding and there was no way I was doing that—I worked his pants low enough on his hips so I could pull him free. His cock jerked in my fist, daring me to stroke.

I swallowed hard.

"Losing your nerve?" he said. Somehow, this had turned into a game, and I was more than ready to play.

"No. I was just making sure I followed your instructions of keeping my hands on you."

With a tight grip on his cock, I tugged and fell to my back. He had no choice but to follow. He caught his weight, his hands landing on the mattress on either side of my head, bracing himself so his big body didn't crash down on mine.

"What do you want from me, Megan?"

"Right now?" I gave a tentative stroke. "Everything you've got. No holding back."

An evil grin split his face. "Done."

He tore my shirt away and yanked my bra off with one hard rip, instantly bearing my breasts. The cool air didn't even have time to hit my flesh before his mouth latched onto my nipple. I skimmed my hands up his body and wove my fingers in his hair. When he bit down on the sensitive peak, I cried out and arched my back for more.

He paid the same attention to the other. Nipping the plump flesh of my entire breasts, as if eating me alive. The only move I could make was to grip him tighter as he raked his mouth along my body, tasting and sampling every square inch from the bottom of my ribcage to the base of my neck. Pulling more of my skin between his lips, he kissed down my throat and along my collar, but always ending on the swell of my breasts, delivering one last bite to my throbbing nipples.

"You taste like sunshine and raspberries." He opened his mouth, skating his teeth down the center of my chest to my navel and leaving a slightly welted trail of teeth marks. "Ripe and warm…I could eat you."

He looked up my body to catch my gaze. He flicked the edge of my panties with his tongue and smiled against the lace. My breaths were coming so quickly I could barely keep up with my lungs.

Looping a finger around the crotch of my panties, he tugged until I heard the quick screech of lace ripping. He pulled away the tattered material, leaving me in nothing but my stockings. His hot mouth closed around the soft spot of my inner thigh and he sucked hard.

"Christ, you're fucking mouth-watering," he growled against my skin.

My blood was boiling and satisfaction surging. That was the growl I had been waiting for. No niceties. No polite words. Raw and unchained lust.

His breath danced over my aching core and I arched. Begging him to taste me where I desperately needed him. Instead, he drew away from me and stood. A clanking and rustling noise rang out as he shucked his pants completely and knelt at the foot of the bed. He grabbed the back of my knees and yanked me toward him until my ass was almost entirely hanging off the edge of the mattress. He spread my legs wide and barely brushed his lips over my clit. My hips jolted upward, seeking more.

"You have the prettiest pussy I've ever seen." He didn't say anymore. Just tossed my legs over his shoulders and buried his face between my thighs.

His tongue darted out and flicked the tangled bundle of nerves, fast and hard. A hot flush clapped my body and I arched into him.

"Yes!" I gripped the sheets at my side and arched.

"Ah-ah," his words vibrated against my aching flesh, "remember the rule?"

I looked down and saw those green eyes staring at me, demanding and angry. I was supposed to be touching *him*. I let go of the sheet and placed my palms tentatively on his head.

A low rumble broke from his chest. He sounded pleased. I had never touched a man's head while doing this before. It seemed so…erotic.

"Good. Now hang on tight, sweetheart," he rasped.

His palms slapped down on my thighs and he tugged me even closer to him. There was no other area on him I could reach. I had no choice but to keep my hands where they were.

He licked the entire length of my sex. I wound my fingers in his hair. He seemed to like that. Keeping his intense green gaze on mine, he took another taste. My grip tightened, so he did it again, and again, until he was raining wet flicks over my pussy, building a fire in my bloodstream.

All inhibitions gone, I pulled his thick hair and dug my heels into his back. I wiggled and moved to try to get him deeper, closer. My entire body was humming and pulsing with liquid nitrogen, the pressure so intense it made my toes tingle. The pleasure was so hot, it felt cold. I was so close…

He released me, quickly grabbed a condom from his discarded pants, rolled it on, and crawled up my body. Adrenalin burst though my veins and lit up every cell. The need to burn this energy and ride him was overwhelming.

I pushed on his chest and he turned to his side. Letting me maneuver him to his back, I straddled his hips. His big cock jutted between us. I leaned down and cupped his face in my palms like I had at the door when he first kissed me.

Slowing the pace just slightly, I explored his mouth with my tongue, taking laps, followed by little nips of his full bottom lip. He cupped my ass and ground his dick against my clit. It was obvious this man was dominant. Probably never laid back and took any-thing, but right now, I wanted to show him all I was feeling. Take out my pent-up aggression on the body he was offering. He was the one who asked me up and he was the one who made the move. I was ready to execute the deal.

Never speeding up the kiss, I subtly moved my hips until I was able to position the tip of his cock at my entrance.

"You know," I whispered against his mouth, "I think you're a lovely man, Preston."

I slammed down on him. My pussy instantly encasing him and we both cried out. His vice grip encased my hips, fingers digging into the bone.

"Fuck, woman." His muscles were all bunched and chorded and I ran my fingers down the flanks of well-cut abdomen.

He lifted my body so that just the tip of his cock was breach-ing me. His hips shot up just as he pulled me down on him. A sharp gasp burst from my throat.

"You're so big," I breathed.

Bracing my weight and sticking to the "constant touch" rule, I pushed on his chest and whipped my hips in his lap. Taking him deep, then stirring until the crown brushed that sensitive spot inside over and over. I was ready to scream from the pleasure.

"Not yet, sweetheart," he grated. The edge of need and ven-geance in his voice made my skin prick. "I'm not done with you yet."

Without severing our connection, he flipped me to my back. He pushed his knees against my thighs, parting them even wider, and thrust again.

"Oh, yes!" I wrapped my legs around him.

He snaked one arm beneath my lower back and pulled me against him. He was rough, deep and ungodly amazing. Every forceful move and sharp thrust was controlled and manipulated so that every nerve ending of his hit mine. The man made love like it was an art and I was falling hard and fast. The burning beneath my bones spread from my core to my fingertips until I couldn't register anything but him.

His scent. His body. His skin. It was the only thing that existed.

He pumped in and out of me, that thick cock stretching me more and more each time. He grew harder with every push and retreat. With one arm around my back the other came up to fist the sheets by my head. His slick chest pressed into my breasts and the feel of our raging heartbeats pounding against each other was almost too much to take.

Weaving his fingers in my hair, he forced my stare to meet his, and silently commanded me not to sever eye contact.

I held on tight. My nails sinking in to his shoulder blades, I kept his gaze.

"Megan…" he whispered my name and for some reason, the tender endearment made my chest hurt and a ping of wetness rise from my tear ducts.

My body erupted. Every atom burst into flames and spiraled from the center of my body to the tips of my toes. I came apart. Yelling his name and begging for more. He gave it. My orgasm was stronger, longer, than any kind of pleasure I'd ever experienced and he drew it out to the edge of the abyss.

When I felt him twitch inside me and the back muscles beneath my palms tighten, it was then I felt it. His release. His grip on me tightened and he buried himself over and over, riding out his own end.

My body was spent and my mind in worse shape than my liquefied bones. Never moving too far away, he pulled out of me and disposed of the condom. I went to sit up, but his arm came around my stomach and snatched me back.

Burrowing his face in the curve of my neck, he fell instantly asleep, holding me like I was something he didn't want to leave.

2

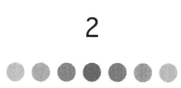

"You look like hell."

I froze with my heels in one hand, the other on the front door knob to my apartment. It was barely eight AM, and after I had peeled the strong, deliciously smelling, Mr. Suit off me and snuck out of the penthouse, I came straight home to what should have been an empty apartment. "What are you doing home? I thought you had work today."

"I do." Emma stood behind the couch, shoving her laptop into her bag. Her long brown hair was pulled up into a high pony-tail and she was dressed in jeans and a yellow shirt. Everything about Emma screamed, "sweet" and "dainty," but the petite bru-nette could out-drink and out-cuss a sailor. She was a freelance programmer and aside from my daily calls to Kate, Emma was my close friend and chat buddy. So I had never been so happy to hear the words, "I'm just running late."

Emma looked up, her big brown eyes going wide and taking in my hair, last night's clothes, and the obvious lack of bra under my blouse. "Oh my God, you're doing the walk of shame."

"What?" I gasped.

"You are! The hair, the I-just-had-an-orgasm glow, and is that—" Emma looked closer and I slapped my hand over my neck. "Is that a hickey?"

"No." It wasn't. "It's teeth marks. And I had three orgasms."

"Three." Emma took a seat and abandoned packing. "I want all the details. So spill." Then her smile faded and she went serious. "Wait. Is this about Brain?"

"No," I said too fast.

She raised a brow. "Really? Because you aren't really a one-night stand kind of girl."

"How do you know?" I asked because she was the second person in the past twelve hours to imply that.

"Because I used to be one and, trust me, you are not. So the fact that you had, what I am assuming was your virgin sail on the USS No-Strings, the same day that Brian elopes with the slut he cheated on you with has me worried."

I sighed and sat on the couch next to her. She was right. I wasn't the one-night kind of person. But for a night it had been fun, thrilling even. "It just sort of happened."

"So, what exactly happened?" she asked with a smile and wag of her brows.

"I found out about Brian and Grace eloping, my mom texted and I guess my dad is getting worse." I shrugged. "It was just one of those days. Then Mr. Preston came in—"

"*Mister* Preston?"

"I didn't really get his first name. We didn't share a lot of info." I closed my eyes and pictured how he looked when I'd snuck out this morning. Stubble on his face, his hair messed from my hands, a small contented smile on his face, and that incredible body, naked for my viewing pleasure. "He came into the bar when I was heading out and we just kind of, clicked."

"Are you going to see him again?"

"No," I said. "He is a client, an important one by his room, and dating clients is against corporate policy."

"What if he wants to see you again?"

Last night was amazing. But like the early spring sun blaring through the window, reality hit hard.

"Can't happen. I could lose my job." Not to mention the fact that I had a one-night stand and didn't even know the guy's full name. That could be a good thing though. He was just passing through. A jetsetter who held meetings in big cities and was gone before the week was through.

He had flicked a switch in me that disregarded consequence and gave way to stupid hormones. It had been so nice shedding all the stress for just one night.

The way he looked at me...as though he wanted to devour me. No one had ever looked at me like that, and it felt good. Still, I knew better than to jeopardize my career, especially when my parents depended on my paychecks.

"I need this job, Emma. I can't afford to mess it up, no matter how sexy the guy is."

"Well, that depends," Emma tapped her chin. "How sexy are we talking?"

I couldn't hide the stupid grin on my face. "Really sexy."

She shrugged. "Then I think it was worth it. No offense, but you've been walking around like a zombie of misery and this is the first time I've seen you smile since I moved in. Everyone needs a break from reality every once in a while."

I looked at my hands. I did need a break. Something in Preston's eyes, in the way his heat surrounded me, and how the smell of him had every reasonable thought scattering out the window.

Getting lost, feeling alive, breaking the rules, I just needed it. Needed him. Truth be told I felt a little lighter this morning. But it was morning, and time to get back to my life.

Another soothing breath. How many times had I told my best friend Kate to just breathe? It was time I took my own advice and calm my nerves. In the middle of a perfect inhale, my phone rang.

I hustled to snatch it from my purse. Caller I.D. said it was the hotel.

"Hello?"

"Hi, Megan, it's Brooke. I need you to come in this afternoon please."

"Ah, it's my day off."

Emma picked up her backpack and mouthed, "Gotta run. See you later," and winked.

I nodded as she slipped out the door.

"Yes, well, something important has come up and I need you to come in at noon," Brooke continued.

My blood froze. They knew. Somehow I'd had been caught and now I was going to lose my job. Bile rose in my throat. Had Mr. Suit told? Complained?

"I can't today." I really couldn't. My dad's specialist had agreed to call me at one o'clock and give me an update on yesterday's appointment. My mom was counting on me and I couldn't risk not getting back in time.

"I suggest that you find the time." Brook lowered her voice and it sounded like she was cupping her hand around the phone. "The request came from high up."

"You mean Bill?"

Bill Chappie was the general manager and never took time to converse with the lowers unless there was a problem. And apparently there was one and it started in the penthouse.

"No, Megan," Brooke whispered. "I mean corporate. And it was red-flagged."

Oh God…

My body shook slightly and I clutched the phone against my ear.

"N-noon is fine."

"Good. And good luck."

The line when dead, and so did my blood pressure.

● ● ●

"He wants you to meet him in his office," Brooke said when I walked up to the front desk.

"Who wants me in what office?"

Brooke looked around and then lowered her voice. Though she and I technically had the same job title, she was twenty years older and had a mother hen vibe, which was oddly comforting.

"Mr. Strauss. He's in *his* office in *his* hotel asking for you."

"The office upstairs?"

She nodded.

John Strauss held office hours at this hotel maybe four times a year. I had never actually seen him but he was rumored to be a nice man in his seventies with white hair.

The only other thing I knew was that he apparently never let anyone know when he decided to randomly drop in. As Brooke so kindly pointed out, it was his hotel—one of the many—so it should be no surprise. But my shock came from the timing. The Strauss office was on the same floor as the penthouse. Last night, I had actually looked at the door on the opposite end of the hall while I was being kissed down by Preston.

My stomach plummeted and I could actually feel my face pale. Was John Strauss in his office last night? Did he arrive early this morning? Maybe he saw me sneak out? The options were limitless but the end result would likely be the same: my termination.

"Did he say why he wanted to see me?"

Brooke looked up from the computer. "He just said to call you in because he needed to discuss an issue about last night."

All the breath coaching in the world couldn't help my lungs in that moment. Because no matter how hard I tried, I couldn't freaking breathe. I tucked a lock of hair behind my ear hoping the small task would stop the trembling in my fingers. It didn't.

I ran my palms down the front of my pants and adjusted my sweater. I wasn't in my normal business skirt and button-up but I still looked better than casual. Thank goodness because apparently I had to go face Mr. Strauss.

"Thanks, Brooke."

I walked down the corridor and turned the corner. There was a private hall with several business rooms, one of which was where we held our staff meetings. I used the express elevator at the back of the office and headed to the top floor where Mr. Strauss had his office. At this rate, I was praying I wouldn't run into Preston since check-out was at eleven.

Coming face to face with the office door, I chanced a look over my shoulder at the penthouse entrance. Funny how a panel of white wood, a brass doorknob and some shiny hinges made my knees weak. Of course, the memories that accompanied that door also escalated my heart rate. I looked back at the task before me, banishing last night from my mind the best I could, and knocked on the office door.

A low voice called out, instructing me to enter.

Deep breath, I reminded myself.

Walking in, I kept my eyes on the floor. No matter how many times I tried to look confident, I ended up feeling—

"Guilty." Mr. Strauss' voice rang out.

"Excuse me?" I looked up and—

Oh. Holy. God.

"I said, *guilty* Miss Riley. You look guilty. Tell me, have you done something wrong?"

My mouth hung open and I gaped, because standing behind a massive mahogany desk in a sleek three-piece suit and perfectly combed dark hair was—

"Preston? I thought I was here to see Mr. Strauss."

He folded his arms and grinned wide. Apparently I missed the joke. Which was what this had to be. A joke.

"I am John Preston Strauss."

"But...you're not old."

He smirked. "You must be thinking of my father, John Charles Strauss. Either that or my older brother John Charles Junior."

"Wait, you all are named John?"

"I think after last night you're safe to call me Preston," he said with a wink.

I reminded myself to ask my mother later if I was born with a heart arrhythmia because what was going on in my chest felt like a war zone. Between shock and awe lay a meltdown, and I was on the brink of losing it.

"Sit," he said and motioned to the chair on the other side of the desk. He took his seat gracefully as I fumbled into mine.

Words! I needed words. But the only thing that came out of my mouth was, "I ah…I'm—"

"You left," he interrupted my mumbling. "You left me last night."

That wasn't what I was expecting him to say. There was no emotion behind the declaration indicating he cared either way. Just a mere statement of events.

I had no idea what to make of this guy or his motives. But I thought we had both been clear on what last night was. A one-time thing. And technically I had left early this morning, but judging by the look on his face that fact wouldn't help my case.

"Forgive me, Mr. Strauss, but isn't leaving the protocol?"

"Again with the rules." He grinned and rested his elbow on the chair's armrest and placed his face between his thumb and first finger. "And, yes, it is. I just find it odd. Usually, I don't fall asleep before I see a woman out."

"Lucky me," I said, then snapped my mouth shut.

This whole thing was effed up to say the least and I was treading very dangerous water. The more the moment sank in and the shock wore off, the more I realized the truth. He knew I was an employee and still asked me back to his room. This had been a set-up. He seduced me dishonestly and on purpose.

"Whatever it is that has you sporting that angry scowl," he waved his finger in the direction of my face, "I suggest you stop."

My anger flared. The same feelings I had been running from—the feelings this man had made me forget—were crashing into me full force. I was lied to, deceived and played. Again. And one stupid decision had landed me on the opposite side of the desk from my "boss" as he sat there holding my future in his hands.

No way. Not this time. Not again.

"Is this a joke? Some sick game you play with your employees?"

"No." His tone was harsh and I felt like I had just overstepped.

Yes, I was mad and ready to fight, defend, do what I had to do to stifle my way out of this mess, but circumstances or not, Preston was imposing as hell. And every bit as sexy as I remembered.

Though he clearly shaved, his strong jaw smoother looking that last night, his eyes were still a vibrant green made more dazzling in the bright light filtering through the large windows. Crisp and cut in his perfectly tailored suit, his body radiated every bit of strength and finesse as it had last night. Calm, controlled and confident as sin. He knew it and I knew it. The only question now: What was his angle?

"Why am I here, Preston?"

"You rushed off so quickly I figured I owed you a proper good morning." Again, I couldn't detect a hint of emotion in his statement. Was he kidding? Serious?

"It's the afternoon and I was getting along just fine without the sentiment." I crossed my arms trying really hard to ignore the stupid smirk on his face, the first indication that he was clearly loving this.

He infuriated me. I came to New York for a fresh start and a good job. I thought I had a no strings, one-night stand and now here I was staring down what could be another huge mistake. In the end, I only had myself to blame, but he could have been honest about who he was. And what was even more annoying was the way my body tingled and sent all the good parts into hyper drive with one flash of his green eyes.

"You said you were just passing through."

"It's my hotel," he sat back, "and I think I'll stay in town for a bit."

"Am I fired?"

"Why would I fire you?"

"Because you tricked me into sleeping with you and—"

"Tricked?" He sat forward and rested his forearms on the desk. "If memory serves you *begged* me to fuck you."

All the air in my lungs burned and I couldn't let go of the breath I was holding.

"Like I said," he continued, obviously happy he had rendered me speechless. "I'll be staying for a while. Due to recent developments, it's clear my staff needs a more hands-on approach in management."

"I am management," I grated between clenched teeth, my mind flashing back to last night.

"Yes, you are. And I can see why we get such high ratings in hospitality."

My blood boiled out of control, my vessels serving no more purpose than a pressure cooker. Embarrassment flooded and every pore was tainted with confusion. Had he called me in to simply mock me?

No way was I going to be the butt of another joke, let alone another man.

"You know what," I stood up, "I'm an adult and proud of the person I am. I'm not the type of girl who makes a habit of having a one-night stand but last night I did, and that's all you were. If you want to try to make me feel bad or cheap about that, you're wasting your time. So either fire me or get over it."

The slightest grin tugged at his lips. "Was I your first?"

"What?" I snapped.

"Was I your first promiscuous sexual encounter?"

I bit my lip to keep the truth from spilling out. Yes, he was. He was actually the only encounter other than my ex Brian. And that one night had been more amazing than all two years put together with Brian.

"I'll take that as a yes," he said. "Now, it is neither my intention to fire or degrade you. But I must admit, I'm exceedingly angry with you."

"Why?" The question came out as a stunned whisper.

"I am your boss, I have made an attempt to be honest with you and have a conversation, yet you tell me I was nothing more than a single night." He pouted a little, which I didn't buy for a second. "That's hurtful you know."

I wanted to roll my eyes, but I was balancing somewhere between fear and awe. He was harsh and dominant, yet had a seemingly easygoing personality. But I didn't know how far that humor went. It was like walking on a mirror slicked with oil, any second you could either slip and cut yourself or fall on your ass. Either way, it was going to be messy.

"I'd like you to dine with me tonight."

I frowned. "I don't think that's a good idea."

"Why?"

"With all due respect, Mr. Strauss, you're my boss and as I said before, I'm not that type of girl. What happened last night was a fluke. I don't normally act like that."

"Are you dumping me?"

"What? No, I—"

The smiled playing on his face stated that he was obviously toying with me.

"You intrigue me, Megan. I'd like to have a meal with you."

I shook my head.

"Why? Because you're not 'that kind of girl'? Then tell me, what kind of girl are you?"

I decided to go with honesty because at this point, the only thing I had left to save was my job.

"I'm the kind that likes relationships built on trust and respect. Where both people know what they're getting into." I paused and glared at him for good measure. "And I want a legitimate connection."

He nodded as if thinking over an offer. "These are practical terms."

"What? I didn't mean—I wasn't proposing any terms."

"You know the one thing I find odd about this whole situation, Miss Riley?"

"You find only one thing odd?"

"You don't seem to care who I am."

Oh God, here we go. I get it. He had probably a billion dollars and hotels around the world and blah, blah, blah. Lots of people had money and things. The fact that he owned the hotel I currently worked at—thus having power over my job—didn't sit well. But beyond that, no, I didn't care. Money had never intimidated me. Besides, I had been around Adam, Kate's fiancé, a lot and he was as rich and domineering as they came.

"No, I don't care who you are, Mr. Strauss."

He nodded. "You've given me a lot to consider. I'll be in touch Miss Riley." I opened my mouth to argue again but he cut me off. "Unless the next words out of your mouth are, 'Yes, Preston, I'd love to have dinner with you tonight,' then you can see yourself out."

3

"Mom?

"Hi Honey, I'm here," my mother's voice rang out over the line.

The cab took a hard right, weaving through afternoon traffic as I headed back to my apartment. It wasn't the ideal place to take the call, but I was happy I hadn't missed it.

"I'm on the line as well, Megan," Dr. Forman said. "I've been speaking with your mother and wanted to share your father's prognosis."

"Okay." I chewed my thumbnail and stared blankly at the back of the blue driver seat.

Lukewarm terror slugged through my veins and my fingers felt cold. Fear. Pure fear was slowly simmering.

"Your father's cognition is rapidly changing and worsening. The rate of decay I detected after examining him has me leaning toward vascular dementia."

"And what does that mean? Is it treatable? I read that dementia can be treated in some cases."

The doctor's long pause didn't do much for my confidence in hoping that my father would—could—get better.

"Megan, vascular dementia is typically caused by a series of small strokes."

"But my dad has never had a stroke."

"Yes, he has, honey. We just thought it was best, with everything else going on, to…we didn't want to worry you." My mother's voice was strained and I could hear it in her tone that she was blaming herself.

My eyes burned and I focused harder on the small blue stitching in front of me to keep from breaking down.

"The strokes have caused vascular lesions in his brain," the doctor went on.

"Can you treat him for that?" I asked.

"Unfortunately, the lesions, like your father's dementia itself, are irreversible."

My heart sunk so low I couldn't feel its pulse in my ribcage anymore.

"But, preventative care in these situations is essential. While the damage has been done, we can monitor and treat your father in the hopes that we can help prevent any further strokes."

"So, that's a positive thing," I whispered, trying to grasp onto any piece of good news I could get.

"Yes, it is," my mother said.

She must be thinking the same thing I was. Preventative care, treatment and constant monitoring equaled expensive.

I shook my head. Whatever it took to make sure my father received the best medical care, I would do. Whatever the cost.

"Will he continue to get worse? With his memory?" I asked.

"I am sorry to say that he will likely continue down this path. However, with treatment, we can slow the process significantly. He will have good days where he is likely to understand everything, recognized everyone and nothing seems amiss. There will also be bad days where he can be extremely disoriented. Of course, there will also be many days where it is somewhere in between. The brain is a powerful, sensitive machine. But catching this now and starting treatment is the best thing for him."

"Of course," my mother whispered.

"Okay," I agreed.

"Also, based on what your mother has been telling me, and the behavior of your father when he is at his worst, an in-house health care provider wouldn't be a bad idea."

My throat hurt. My mother had been keeping the details of my father's progression from me if the doctor was thinking it was bad enough to have daily medical help.

"Thank you so much, Dr. Forman. I really appreciate you talking with me today."

"Absolutely, Megan. I understand you're living in New York so I will discuss the details of treatment with your mother, but don't hesitate to call if you have questions."

"Thank you," I said again.

"I'll hang up and let you ladies talk."

A click sounded over the line. "You still there, Mom?"

"Yes, I'm here."

"Why didn't you tell me about Daddy?" I tried to keep the hurt out of my voice, but it was impossible.

"Like I said, we didn't want to worry you." My mother wasn't a dishonest woman, she just omitted the truth when she didn't want to speak about things. Whenever she was vague, it usually meant she was hiding something. And for the past few months, vague didn't even begin to describe her.

My chest ached with guilt. I should have known that things were getting worse. Should have been more persistent in my questions, because after hearing Dr. Forman's diagnosis, things were not fine.

"Well, I am beyond worried, so please tell me the truth. Are you okay?"

"No, I'm not, honey. I don't like my daughter sending me money every month." There was a slight sob laced on the last word and it broke my heart.

"Mom, don't be upset. I want to help. It's my fault you're in the situation in the first place."

"You stop that right now, Megan Marie. You did nothing wrong."

"I convinced you to risk your house, your retirement in something that I should have known was too good to be true, and I lost it."

"Oh, Megan," her voice was so soft, so understanding, so worried. She had never blamed me. Never yelled. Not once. Not even when they lost everything. "Tim was the one who cheated us. You were trying to help. I don't want to hear you say otherwise again."

I lowered my head and pinched the bridge of my nose, trying to keep the tears behind my eyes where they belonged. She didn't want to fight with me about this the same way I didn't want her to fight with me about the money. I knew what I sent to her was just enough to keep the house out of foreclosure…barely.

Between the needed daily help with my dad and his new treatments, the mountain of needs was far outweighing the means. If we had to look into hiring a live-in nurse—because there was no way my dad would function in a nursing home where everything was new and unfamiliar—I had a feeling things were on the verge of changing for the worst.

"I love you, Mom." It was the only way to end this conversation. Arguing with her right now wouldn't do anything. Both of them were tired and scared and needed time to process everything they'd just been told.

"I love you too."

"Can I talk to Daddy?"

"Of course." There was a pause then my father came on the line.

"Hello?"

"Hi, Daddy!"

"Who's on the line?" he asked.

I heard my mother mumble something in the background. I didn't hear it clearly, but it sounded like she was trying to explain who I was.

"What? No, there's no Megan here."

"No, Daddy. I'm Megan."

"I think you have the wrong number."

My skin surged tight and my chest suddenly felt like it was trying to support steel weights instead of my lungs.

"Daddy, it's me, Megan. Your daughter"

"I'm sorry, honey. Your father is really tired right now." My mother sounded flustered and upset.

"He doesn't remember me, does he?" I tried to keep the words steady, but it was no use. The other day when he'd called me Fresca, he had rallied quickly. But it was different this time. There was no recognition in his voice.

"Of course he does. He just…he just has good and bad days. You heard what Dr. Forman said, some days this just happens."

I nodded even though she couldn't see me. My entire body hurt as though all my limbs had fallen asleep. My father was forgetting me.

"Tell him I love him," was all I could choke out. "I'll call you later."

"Okay, honey."

I hung up and bit the inside of my cheek hard enough to taste blood, clamped a palm over my forehead and let the pain of the truth sink in.

My father's mind was dying and I couldn't do anything to help.

My mother and the doctor would speak later this week about treatments and schedules and I couldn't shake the feeling that I was sending her into a gun battle holding a knife. Money, insurance—we didn't have either—would be questions I didn't want her to face alone.

The cabbie continued to weave through downtown Manhattan and I looked out the window, praying for a miracle and hoping to hell Preston meant what he said and wouldn't fire me. I needed my job now, more than ever, and yet, remembering his warm arms wrapped around me sounded really good right now.

I leaned my head against the window, settling for a cold piece of glass against my cheek.

* * *

"Could have been worse news," Emma said handing me a glass of wine and sitting on the couch next to me. "They can help him. That's something." Her voice was soft and soothing and yes, she was right. Slowing down the process was better than nothing.

"Yeah, I know." I drank my wine in one long, long gulp.

"Holy hell, girl. Slow down, you're making me look bad," Emma said.

"Can we talk about something else?" I just needed to let everything sink in and talking about my dad right now was not something I wanted to go into.

"Of course," Emma poured more wine into my glass and took a swallow of her own. Her long brown hair was in a messy bun on the top of her head and since she had taken her contacts out for the evening, she shoved her dark rimmed glasses up her nose. "How about we talk more about Mr. Sexy turning out to be your boss? I still can't get over it!"

Yeah, that was a doozy. "Not just my boss, Preston is the owner."

"Still calling him Preston, huh? Not 'Mr. Strauss?' " Emma teased.

I smiled. It was such a laid-back name. Not nearly as intimidating as John Preston Strauss. The man oozed self-assurance and all his alpha male swagger and charm had worked on me. There was no denying it now. Problem was, I couldn't figure out how to move on from here.

"He's different. Like there's different sides of him. Last night I saw the dominant aggressive side and today it was like talking to a playful frat boy."

"God, I love frat boys." Emma sighed and swirled her wine glass. "He seems honest though. And he could have let you get away but he didn't."

"Don't start with that."

"What? All I'm saying is it's kind of romantic."

I groaned and took a sip of wine. The idea of kids and house and doting husband had always been my end goal. Hell, part of me still wanted that. But for me, that particular table had turned, stranding me at the corner of Crap and Oh-shit Street.

Several months ago I had encouraged my best friend Kate to go after Adam. He had nearly hit her with his car and border-line stalked her but I had never seen Kate so at peace. Somehow, Adam had broken through all her walls and made the light shine through my best friend. If Kate's anxiety had a cure, it was Adam Kinkade.

While no one deserved happiness more than Kate, the idea of "happy endings," was long gone from my list of possibilities. Emma, however, tended to like the elaborate romance idea, though she'd never admit it. Her collection of Nicolas Sparks' movies were a dead giveaway.

"I'm over the romantic thing. I'm honestly wondering if it even exists." I wasn't trying to be negative, just realistic. My parents were an amazing example of love and commitment. Kate and Adam were well on their way to sunshine and rainbow town. A place that was lost on me.

Reality trumped any fictional desires of happiness that Brian hadn't managed to destroy. Moving to New York had been my first step in letting go of the idea that love, marriage, and babies were my happily ever after. My family was struggling, and that was my focus.

Besides, relationships apparently weren't my strong point. I had dedicated the last two years to a guy who, not only didn't see forever when he looked at me, but also left me feeling little better than a fool. And while I never did anything with my ex-boss, Tim, he threw, not only me, but my parents under the bus. Trust, men, and emotions didn't go together. Not in my world.

"If I ever meet the boy that did this to you I'm going to bitch slap him," Emma said, as if pulling my thoughts out of my mind.

"He's not worth it, trust me."

"Yeah, well, he and his skanky lady can just rot in Chicago together. You have bigger and better things going on."

Emma's encouragement did help. While I kept the details about my parents' financial situation to myself, she obviously knew about Tim going to jail and the scam, as well as Brian and Grace. But she was right. I did have a good thing going here. Well, better than what I had going in Chicago.

I always wanted a career of my own in business or finance. I had moved up quickly at the hotel and was making decent money. I was also in the greatest city in the country and had good friends and great parents. I was better without Brian. I knew that. But the residual crap left over from a cheating asshole ex-boyfriend and thieving felon for a former boss really shook my confidence. I always thought I was a great judge of character, now I had a hard time trusting my judgment on what to order for lunch.

"Okay, enough about this." Emma clapped her hands. "Tell me more about today. After the one-night stand."

I smiled and told her what Preston had said earlier.

"And you turned him down?"

"There was nothing to accept."

"You said he asked you to dinner."

"Yeah, but I couldn't tell if he was serious or playing a game. And either way, it's not a good idea. What if we go out, and it doesn't work, then he fires me? Or worse, I am stuck needing a job that reports to a guy who I have a 'history' with? Talk about awkward."

"Good point. I think powerful men like that always have an agenda, but Meg, he wouldn't have asked you in if he didn't at least like you a little bit. He could have his pick of women and he called you."

"Thanks a lot," I grumbled.

"You know what I mean. You're hot and you're funny and I'm sure you kick ass in the sack."

"I just don't get it. He offered dinner, then somehow turned it around on me. Like twisted my words and made me feel like I was the one who was approaching him with something." I shook my head.

"Yep, that's called the Jedi-Mind-Trick." She took a drink of her wine. "The douche 2.0 version is the worst."

I smiled. Preston wasn't mean, or an ass. Well, kind of…but not in an overly assy way. I pinched my nose, even my thoughts were sounding lame.

"Do you like him?"

I considered that for a moment. He was irritating. Intense. Handsome. Sexy as hell and the way he moved his strong body so fluidly over mine was something out of a Greek god training manual. He was definitely rocking some good aspects. But, a single fact remained that I couldn't ignore.

"He owns the hotel I work in. Tell me that's not a bad idea."

"Oh, that's a terrible idea," Emma instantly agreed. "But that's not what I asked." Heat stained my cheeks. "I knew it! You have it bad for him."

"Do not."

"I can see it on your face."

39

"A night of good sex after a drought can do that," I defended.

"So it was good?"

It was beyond good. Everything about Preston was new and unexpected. Yet I instantly felt comfortable with him. If I didn't, I wouldn't have slept with him or spoken to him the way I had earlier today.

"It doesn't really matter. I need to just worry about keeping my job."

Emma held out his wine glass and clanked it against mine. "Well if anything, I'd say you earned a raise."

4

"Is there something you want to say?" Brooke asked and handed me a note.

It was Monday afternoon and I had just walked into the hotel to relieve Brooke and start my shift. It had been a long weekend and I was anxious to occupy my mind outside the four walls of my apartment.

"Excuse me?" I took the note from her and unfolded the piece of paper.

Have Miss Riley come to my office first thing when she arrives.

~ J.P. Strauss

I glanced up to see Brooke smiling at me.

"What's going on with you and Mr. Strauss?"

"Nothing."

She raised her brows. I straightened my stance, made sure my usual black pencil skirt and white button-up was crisp and neat, and made the long walk to the office, and person, I had been dreading all weekend. Of course that dread was interrupted by bouts of daydreaming and naughty thoughts, but still.

I wasn't even out of earshot when whispers instantly began circling behind the front desk that I was getting fired. My skin broke into a cold sweat and my mouth went dry. Once again, a stupid decision made without adequate research was threatening to bite me in the ass.

How could I have slept with Preston Strauss?

A long elevator ride and too much silence later, I rapped lightly on the office door.

"Good morning, Miss Riley," Preston said, opening the door.

"Hi." I kept my head up, but my eyes averted.

No matter how much courage I tried to muster, I just couldn't bring my gaze to meet his. A single look made me lose focus. Right now, shame was my name and I couldn't lose my job. It wasn't just me counting on the money. There wasn't much I wasn't willing to do to keep my parent in that house, including beg, especially since I had three home-care services call me back with quotes this morning. And it looked as though I'd need to find a second job just to cover the cost of a part-time health-companion, which Medicaid didn't cover.

"Are you unwell?"

I frowned and looked at him. "I'm fine. Ready to start my shift."

"About that." He rounded his desk, and that was when I noticed an older man with light gray hair and a suit that almost swallowed him. "Megan, this is my attorney, Lars Blackman."

"Oh shit," I breathed, and it wasn't until Preston arched a brow at me that I realized I said it out loud.

Lars Blackman was a world-renowned attorney even though he looked like the sweetest thing in the world. At just over five and a half feet tall with small shoulders and wrinkly face, he resembled a Shar Pei. The man was ruthless. I wasn't just getting fired, I was getting annihilated.

"Why don't you have a seat, Miss Riley."

Too shocked and terrified to do anything else, I sat, my skirt hugging tight as I crossed my legs and attempted to sit up straight and not burst into tears. No matter how hard I tried to look put-together and professional, the fact remained that it was this very uniform that had been rumpled and on the floor of Preston's penthouse a few nights ago. I felt like a fraud. Like he could see right through me.

"Care for a drink?" he asked, sitting behind his desk. Mr. Blackman remained standing at his side. Two against one.

"No, thank you."

Preston folded his arms and sat back in his chair. He looked incredible. Dark green button-up with white cuffs and collar. The first two buttons were undone and the dark gray pants and black leather belt completed the "rich and powerful" ensemble. Of course the reputably lethal attorney standing on his right didn't hurt the image either.

Mr. Blackman handed Preston a hefty file folder. He placed it on his desk and threaded his fingers over the top of it.

"I have a proposition for you, Megan."

I folded my lips together and tried not to fidget. "What kind of proposition?"

"A marriage proposition."

My vision went blurry and it took me a good three seconds to realize it was because I was blinking my eyes rapidly. I looked at Mr. Blackman. He was stoic. Perfectly calm and not an ounce of rapture on his face. Then I looked at Preston. Same expression.

"I'm sorry, I don't understand?" My voice was somewhere between a laugh, scoff, and utter confusion.

"I'd like to marry you," he said with no more emotion than explaining the weather.

I had to be hearing him wrong. "But I—don't you mean you want to *fire* me?"

"No. Why would I fire my fiancé?"

"Why would you ask me to be your fiancé?" My heart was pounding and I was pretty sure I was going to pass out. I cupped my throat and tried to manually force myself to swallow. This was either a cruel joke or Preston Strauss was off his meds.

"I've given a lot of thought to your terms and I accept."

"What? Are you crazy?"

"Not that I'm aware of." He looked at Mr. Blackman and the lawyer shook his head, agreeing with Preston's statement.

I was in the twilight zone, and not the kind with the hot tween vampires. No. I'm talking full-blown crazy town.

"You look pale, Megan."

I felt the blood leave my face. "Ah, probably because I'm confused and shocked."

"Well, it's really very simple. I need a wife and you need money. We can help each other. Lars and I have spent the weekend going over everything and I have the contract drawn up and ready to go."

"Whoa." I swayed in my seat and wondered if it was possible to pass out while sitting down. I closed my eyes and placed my palm in her forehead, forcing myself to breathe.

A set of hands cupped my knees and the unexpected feel of rough palms on my skin sent shivers up my thighs. I opened my eyes and found Preston kneeling before me, those blazing greens burning bright with what almost looked like worry.

"Forgive me. I know this is shocking. I'm not good with conversational niceties."

"No kidding?" I murmured. "Seriously, Preston, is this some kind of joke?"

"No. I don't joke about things as important as this."

He gently massaged my knee and my dizzy brain began swimming for a whole other reason. Damn the man. Damn his hands. Damn his voice. Damn his bluntness that made me want to keel over and damn that sexy gleam in his eyes and perfect smile. Damn it all.

"If you're okay to continue, I'll explain."

44

I nodded instantly. "An explanation would be wonderful."

He gave a curt nod then moved to sit behind his desk again.

Mr. Blackwell put a single printed piece of paper in front of me and a pen. "This is a non-disclosure agreement. Whatever we talk about in here stays in here. Any conversation we have will remain private and confidential."

I looked up at the attorney. Again, a mask of seriousness. I took his pen in my hand, trying not to shake. I read over the agreement. Standard non-disclosure. Apparently whatever we were about to talk about was defcon-super-secret-freak-Megan-out kind of info.

I signed and Mr. Blackman took the paper. He nodded to Preston.

"Okay, here's the situation," Preston began. "I hold forty-nine percent of Strauss holdings worldwide."

I nodded. I had heard the typical stories when I started working here, but most of them were about John Strauss Senior. Little was mentioned about his two sons, mostly because they seemed to work behind the scenes and no one had ever really met them.

"My brother, Charlie, holds forty-eight percent." Preston's eyes went hard when he spoke of his brother. There was obviously no love lost there. "And my father owns the remaining three percent."

"Okay," I said in understanding.

"My father is retiring. Though he will sit on the board, he is set to give his three percent stake to either my brother or myself."

Ah, now it made sense. That three percent if given to Charlie would put him at fifty-one percent and the majority over Preston. I had dealt with my fair share of contracts and legal issues in real estate and property management—not to mention several college courses on business and finance.

"I see you've mentally worked through the math."

"Yes, but I still don't see what this has to do with you getting married."

"I have built this hotel into an empire. My brother has merely inherited what he has. My father is aware of this and up until I spoke to him last week, was prepared to give me the three percent. Now, he's leaning toward giving it to Charlie."

"Why?"

"Because he has a legacy," Preston snarled the last word.

It was the first time I saw the angry side start to seep out. There was apparently a lot going on with this family that I didn't know and probably didn't want to. Growing up with Kate as a best friend, I had a firsthand look at her family. Whether they were mentally ill or just plain mean, I learned that appearances can be deceiving.

"Charlie and his wife just had their first child."

"I see." My brain was processing a mile a minute, but at least things were starting to make some sense. Trying to keep things straight, I replayed Preston's words. So Preston wanted the majority of the holdings, but John Charles Senior wanted a Strauss heir, which Preston's brother had, but Preston didn't. "So you want to…"

Boom! My blood pressure spiked when the piece slipped into place.

"Are you saying that you want to have a baby? With me!?"

"No." He sounded more disgusted by the idea than I did, which sort of hurt and was a completely stupid emotion. I barely knew the man. But this situation was proving to exceed anything I ever expected.

"I just want to marry you. We will show everyone that we are a happy, stable couple and that will be enough for presumption that we will have a family."

"But we won't."

"No." He glanced at Mr. Blackwell, then his gaze was back on me. "I'm asking for three years, Megan. Everything will operate as a standard engagement. Then a wedding, and yes," his eyes bore into mine, "consummation of the marriage."

Embarrassment snared through my bones like a freshly hit drum. I looked at Mr. Blackwell, who didn't seem to care in the slightest.

"If you say yes, there will be a prenuptial agreement. During the time of our engagement and marriage, you will be provided for and have a weekly allowance as well as an escrow account of five million dollars that will fund at the end of three years. Then you will take your money and we part amicably."

That shock I had finally pushed down? Rose times ten.

"I…I don't think I can…this is…" I started toying with the hem of my skirt.

"Lars, can you excuse us for a moment?" Preston said.

The attorney quietly left and shut the door behind him.

"Look at me, Megan." My eyes snapped to his like a magnet to metal. "I know this must be a lot to take in, but I'm running out of time. I need you to help me with this and you," he opened the file in front of him, "could benefit from my help as well."

My stomach roiled and my skin felt damp and chilly.

He looked through the papers. "You worked for Tim St. Roy at his real estate firm in Chicago."

Oh no…

What exactly did he have on me? Preston continued, like listing the facts of my life was no big deal.

"St. Roy was imprisoned a few months ago for investment fraud, money laundering and tax evasion. And it looks like," he flipped more pages, "your parents were two of the unlucky victims of his scheme."

A scheme I unknowingly helped him with. I pushed my parents to invest. Thought it would be good for them. They put up their house and sank their retirement into something that I had facilitated, only to lose it all. We were barely able to make the house payments after the second mortgage was taken out on it.

We were sinking. And it was my fault.

"Based on your bank records, it looks like you wire every spare cent you make back to your parents."

I frowned so hard I felt it on the back of my head. "How did you—this is an invasion of privacy."

"When you applied for employment here you consented to a background check."

"Yeah, but this is—"

"Thorough research," he cut in.

I shook my head and for some reason tears started rising to the surface. This was too much. Too weird. How had my life taken such a wrong turn? A year ago I had graduated college with a mission to take on the world, have a husband who loved me and a family that wasn't in financial ruins. Apparently that had been too much to hope for.

Nothing was easy, and the rainbows I had been thinking would somehow shoot out of the world's ass and glitter over my life were long gone. My parents were on the brink of bankruptcy and losing the house I grew up in. My father was the one who taught me to work for what you wanted. But he was losing his mind and I was running out of options. The dreams of happiness and success looked more like a glitchy hologram than a reality.

"Megan," Preston pulled me back to attention. "I have the contract. It's simple and profitable for both of us."

"And you think that if we just play the part of the happy couple your father will give you what you want?"

"Yes."

"What about your brother? Won't he be upset? Won't someone notice that some random girl just popped up out of nowhere?"

"No. I travel a lot and keep my personal life very private. My family doesn't involve themselves in my affairs aside from business."

"But what about your mom? Mom's always know—"

"She died when I was thirteen."

"Oh, I'm sorry."

"That's unnecessary." He shifted in his seat. The issue of his mom was clearly uncomfortable. But he recovered quickly. Calm shoulders and hard face fell back in place. "Charlie may be the first born, but he will sink the company if he gets the majority and my father knows that. The old man is adamant about a damn legacy though."

"But you have no intention of giving him that."

"Doesn't matter. Once we're married, he'll assume we will have children and I won't let him think otherwise. That will be enough."

"This seems so…wrong."

"Does it?" He sat back in his chair in a way I was beginning to recognize. He did this when he held the upper hand. "We are two consenting adults. We're sexually compatible and have something to gain from the other. If more people discussed the pitfalls and terms of this sort of arrangements more marriages would last."

"Yeah, but ours has an expiration of three years, so essentially your point doesn't matter because we'll end in divorce anyway despite our discussion."

He grinned. "Yes, but I can promise that it will be an enjoyable three years."

His voice held a dark edge and his eyes ran down the length of my body. My skin pricked and my breasts tingled, suddenly feeling very heavy. He was not like anything I'd ever encountered. Hard and playful. Blunt and logical. Yet there was an animalistic side that I'd bet rarely got unleashed. I had seen it the other night and my confused body was already grappling for another taste. Which wasn't helpful.

"You said the other day that you wanted three things from a relationship: trust, respect and connection." He counted on his fingers. "You also wanted to know what you were getting into. I've acquiesced to all your requests. I am laying out everything I want and asking you if you agree. No lies. No secrets. You have full disclosure. You also have my respect and it's no secret that we *connect* well."

Good lord, the man was sexy when he smiled. I had to remind myself to stay reasonable.

"And how long will that respect last?"

He grinned. "You mean, will I be faithful to you?"

"No." *Yes.*

"I would view this as a legitimate marriage. Which means yes, I would be faithful and expect the same from you."

I rubbed my temples because I was pretty certain my brain was suffocating from lack of oxygen and misfiring of synapses.

"I just…this is all so clinical."

I heard him move, but didn't look up to follow him. His breath was instantly on the back of my neck. He stood behind me and reached around to place his hands on the armrests of my chair, caging me in from behind.

"Does it help to know that I'm painfully attracted to you?" He moved his head to the other side and kissed my earlobe. "That I have thought of nothing but that night, with you sprawled out beneath me." Kiss. "I can still feel my cock deep inside you." Nip. "Feel your lips on my neck and your nails in my back."

I shuttered out a breath. My whole body was singing and begging for him. I clenched my fists to keep from reaching out.

"We'd make a good couple, Megan. Just because it's unconventional doesn't mean it's clinical."

He drew away and came to stand in front of me, leaning back against the edge of his desk. If I hadn't believed his words, the obvious bulge in his pants would have given him away.

God, I wanted this man. So much that I'd thought of little else. But the rollercoaster of the last few days was wearing me down hard. I came in today expecting to get fired and instead had a marriage proposal and a way to take care of my parents offered to me.

With that kind of money I could afford a full-time nurse.

"Three years, and I can use the money however I want."

He nodded. "The money I give you is yours. The lump sum will be paid out at the end of the contract but, yes, in the meantime, the money I give you weekly is yours to do with as you'd like. Your basic needs, living expenses and the wedding costs I will take care of separately."

"And no children?" I needed to reaffirm that concept.

"No. Actually," he glanced over his shoulder, "should you get pregnant, it will void the contract and you get nothing."

I opened my mouth to say something, but what? I didn't want to have a child with someone I didn't love. I didn't want to argue, but this clause—along with everything else—seemed odd.

It wasn't until I took a deep breath and thought about it, that it began making sense. A child was a tie to someone forever. Child support, legal fees, alimony and God knew what kind of trouble could come from dragging a paternity suit through family court for someone with assets like Preston Strauss.

Too much information was coating my mind. I thought of what my dad would say. A piercing pain stuck me in the ribs. My father wouldn't say much, because he struggled to even remember who I was.

Something very deep and very raw bubbled from the core of my soul and threatened my composure. I always thought my father would be there when I got married. Thought he'd walk me down the aisle and give me away. At the rate things were going, he may not even know me in a few months. Fake wedding or not, this may be the only chance I had for him to be a part of something like this. The realization was icing on this fucked-up cake I was being offered.

I ran a fingertip along my lower lashes, shook off the awful feeling beginning to consume me, and looked at Preston.

"Anything else?"

"I'll need a copy of your medical records before we can begin. Proof of health and preventative contraception measures taken. Mine are already on file."

I stood up and tried to get a handle on my shaking legs. There was a lot to think about and I hadn't entirely made up my mind. Though part of me felt like a glorified prostitute, the other part really heeded what Preston had said.

We were being honest, mapping out what we both wanted and didn't want, and what we stood to gain. We liked each other. Attraction wasn't an issue. People got married for much less. And gold-diggers went about this thing all the time in secret. We were consenting adults discussing a contract.

Yet the mental fight I was waging wasn't one hundred percent convincing. Still, my parents were floundering, and it was my fault. Even at the rate I was going with my job at the hotel, it wasn't enough. My father needed serious care and my mother needed help.

I walked to the door and opened it. Preston was right behind me.

"If I say no, do I still have my job?"

"Of course. What we discussed here today stays between us. Your job will be safe. It's not my desire to make your life difficult."

I looked over my shoulder at him. A soft sincerity tinted his eyes and it hit me like a punch to the gut. There was something about him. And it was suffocating me, forcing me to beg for air only he could provide.

He followed me down the hall. We rode the elevator in total silence and once in the lobby, I faced him. My back was toward the massive front doors and the chill of spring air hit my shoulders as guests walked in and out of the hotel. To my right was the desk I would walk behind and start my shift. I tried not to notice the prying eyes staring at me.

Preston gently grabbed my hand in his and ran his thumb over my knuckles. The action was so sensitive, and so different from the all-business attitude of a few moments ago in his office. He was close enough that I could feel the heat of his body envelop mine and I wanted to reach out and snag that warmth. To find some kind of comfort in this whole mess and gain footing on the life I had been missing for the past six months.

"How long do I have to think about this?" I breathed. It was easy getting caught up in his presence—a fact I was learning the hard way.

He tilted his head down, his lips hovering over mine. I was lost. All I could focus on was his mouth and the memory of how good it felt on me.

He glanced over my shoulder. "About forty-five seconds."

My eyes shot wide. "What? I can't make a decision like this in—"

"Thirty seconds."

"This is crazy!" I whispered harshly. The smile he unleashed turned all my insides to puddles and I knew he had me.

"Is that a yes?"

"When would we start?"

He pulled me into his arms. "Right now," and kissed the breath from me.

5

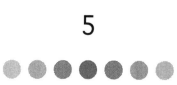

His kiss was firm, but his lips were soft against mine. It was possessive. Controlled. Meant to knock a girl off her feet. And he had succeeded because my knees were weak and the only reason I stayed upright was due to his strong embrace.

He pulled away and barely touched the tip of my nose with his.

"Thank you," he whispered.

I didn't get a single word out because he spun me around to face two very confused-looking men with equally questioning glares.

"Father, how are you?" Preston said and shook the older man's hand while keeping one on the small of my back.

Oh crap!

"Preston," he greeted back, his eyes floating to mine.

He was a tall man and in great shape despite the fact he had to be pushing seventy-five. Preston shared the same strong jaw and broad shoulders, but the older man's eyes were a dim blue while Preston's were a vibrant green—a trait he must have gotten from his mother.

"What is this?" the younger man asked, waving a hand in my direction as if inquiring about a stain on the carpet. "Another one of your pets?"

Preston's hand on my back tightened, fisting the material of my shirt. His stare was locked on the man who, judging by the asshole attitude and blatant insult, was Preston's brother I'd heard so much about.

"I'm Megan Riley," I offered, hoping to defuse the testosterone exchange.

"My fiancé," Preston added with a smirk. "Megan, this is my father John and my brother Charlie."

If Charlie's distaste about my presence wasn't already obvious, the creepy and unwavering glare was a dead giveaway. I tried to swallow the unease flicking up my throat.

"You can't be serious," Charlie said, crossing his arms over his chest. "Don't your women usually stray before you get them locked down?" The grin teasing Charlie's mouth was pure evil. I wasn't exactly following the digs he was throwing, but I did recognize one thing: Preston. And he was pissed.

With a tight grip on me, his body hummed with tension, like any moment he'd shoot out of his skin and rip Charlie's throat out.

"Is there a reason you're being so rude?" I said to Charlie. My parents taught me that if you had a question, ask. They also taught me manners, which Charlie was clearly lacking.

"It's because he's threatened," Preston said, his stare fused on his brother.

Charlie was shorter and not much to look at. His skin was showing signs of his age, which I'd guessed to be early forties. I knew he was older than Preston but I didn't know by how much. Probably because I didn't even know how old my "fiancé" was.

"Well, I think this is splendid!" John said and wrapped me in a hug.

Preston wasn't kidding about him really wanting this legacy. But the tense interaction between his sons—accompanied by

John's obvious avoidance—told me that there was a lot this family buried and didn't deal with.

"When did you two get engaged?"

"Recently." Preston answered his father before I could.

"You should have called," John said to Preston.

"You were in Paris."

"Oh, I hear Paris is beautiful this time of year," I offered, hoping this direction was leading to some kind of pleasant conversation.

"It was," Charlie cut in. "The family reunion was grueling though." He shot a sinister leer at Preston.

I glanced over my shoulder at Preston. "Why didn't you go to the reunion?"

"Because it's not his family," Charlie quipped.

"My, my you're a beautiful young lady," John cut in, once again ignoring Charlie's comments and changing the subject. He held me back with a firm grip on my shoulders to examine me.

I was so lost. John didn't seem to have a mean bone in his body, he also didn't seem to acknowledge the fact that there was a serious rift between the Strauss sons. And what was that about not being Preston's family? Obviously Preston was John's son, so was Junior over there just saying stupid things and being a douche for the hell of it?

"Beautiful?" Charlie's gaze openly slid down my body and I felt the instant need to shower.

Preston stepped toward his brother, shoulders square, a brick tower closing in on an anthill.

"That's enough," John snapped, than instantly returned his attention back to me. "Where are you from, dear?" I looked at Preston with what had to be horror because what the hell was happening? This was the worst conversation ever, if it could even be called that. It felt more like a string of insults laced with a question here and there.

When Preston's death stare finally turned from Charlie and found mine, I watched his chest rise on a deep breath. The look on his face was that of a man who mastered control and obviously practiced in letting certain things go. Vulnerability and raw animosity warred over his expression, and the look broke something in my heart.

I stepped away from John and back toward Preston. Lacing my fingers through his, I gripped his hand and smiled up at him. I didn't know what the issues were, but fake fiancé or not, as long as I was there, he wouldn't face it alone.

"I'm from Illinois," I said, facing John once more. "I grew up on the outskirts of Chicago."

"Beautiful city," John said. He seemed like such a sweet, genuine man and I couldn't help but like him immediately. Preston gave a gentle squeeze and my muscles eased a bit and a touch of relaxation spread through me.

"Well, this is just wonderful news. Why don't we all grab a bite and get caught up," John said.

"Father, we came here for a board meeting. That's it," Charlie grated.

"Megan was just on her way out. She has a doctor's appointment," Preston said. He unwound his fingers from mine. A streak of loss and sadness was quickly replaced when I felt that same hand once again find the small of my back and rest there.

"Nothing serious I hope?" John asked.

"Oh, no." I smiled. Not unless you count marrying your son and gathering proof you're not going to entrap him with a child "serious."

Preston leaned in so his lips were by my ear and whispered so only I could hear, "Get me those medical records and we'll sign the paperwork tonight." His breath against my neck made my knees weak for the millionth time that hour. At this rate, I'd never stand straight in Preston's presence.

He pulled back, his voice a normal pitch. "I'll let Brooke know about your appointment. See you tonight, sweetheart." With that, he slapped my ass.

I stood and gaped at him. He just smiled and John was going to burst with beaming happiness. Junior looked about ready to birth a littler of swamp rats.

"Okay, bye," I said and took a stuttered step toward the exit.

"Nice meeting you, dear," John called.

"You too, sir."

Preston led them in the opposite direction to what, I could only assume, was the board meeting Charlie spoke of.

My heels took a few unsteady clacks against marble as I walked to the front doors. I glanced at Brooke behind the desk. She was silently sending me strength. The woman probably thought I'd just been sacked, instead of sacking the boss.

God, what have I gotten myself into?

6

I sat in the back of the town car and stared out the window. New York really was beautiful. It had been a long day, but after being poked, prodded and examined, Preston's driver picked me up and was en route back to the hotel.

When I left, I hadn't even the time to get my arm up for a taxi before Preston's driver pulled up with strict orders to take me to Preston's personal doctor. Lots of *personal* stuff was going on and apparently all the arrangements had been made, without me, while I was on the way there.

My phone buzzed and I pulled it out of my purse. It was Kate.

"How's Miss Big City doing?" Kate asked.

I missed her the moment I heard her voice. We talked almost every day but it was still a hard adjustment. We'd lived together since college and had been best friends even longer. Leaving her behind had been difficult, but after she and Adam got engaged, I knew it was only a matter of time before she moved out anyway.

"Chicago was a big city," I defended.

"Yeah, but it's not the same thing as New York."

That was true.

"I miss you so much, Meg! Everyone is leaving for spring break and I have nothing to grade and no lectures to give and I just…I miss you."

My heart sank a little. "I miss you too." But *miss* didn't begin to describe it. The last several months had changed my life in such a fundamental way, it was hard to say what I was truly lacking and what I was really aching for.

There was a distance in everything I once held close. Kate was the one person who knew everything about me, the one person I confided in, but after things fell apart and Tim went to jail, I couldn't bring myself to tell her about my parents' involvement, or that all of their money was gone.

Call it shame or pride, I took the best job I could get, determined to fix it on my own. Kate had already been through enough in her life. She would have felt terrible if she knew her uncle cheated my parents. She would have set to make it right. But that was my job, and one I took seriously. Still, keeping pieces of my life secret from the ones I cared about most was tough.

"You can't be too upset about spring break. You have Adam to occupy you," I said, going for a lighter conversation.

She giggled a little. A true, honest sound of bliss. I was so happy for her that she found someone as amazing as Adam. They both had issues to overcome but I'd never met two people more perfect for each other.

"That's true. Speaking of Adam, it looks like his firm has a job opening—"

"Kate, I can't. We've been over this. I learned the hard way that working for family is not a good idea. You and I are family."

"I know, I just...it makes sense. With both you and Emma there, things aren't the same. You'd get great money and honestly, you wouldn't have to worry about a thing."

That was the problem, I needed to worry. I was responsible not only for myself but all my mistakes, which unfortunately affected my parents. If I were being honest, Chicago was a place I loved, the place I grew up, but I wasn't ready to go back. Too much awfulness still lingered there. When I returned, I would be strong and set this whole mess right.

Besides, it was looking like I'd be in New York for the next three years anyway—not a hard price to pay when it meant my father got a live-in nurse and my mother kept the house she loved.

"I want to hear about you. Have you set a date yet?" My tone was chipper even though everything else about me was exhausted.

Kate sighed and thankfully let me change the subject.

"Not yet. Adam's getting kind of grouchy about it."

"I bet. Can't keep stringing the guy along, you know."

She laughed. "Oh please. I'm in it for the long haul. I just don't see the rush. Between the stuff with Tim and the custody battle for Simon, I'd like everything to die down. I want to get married when there are no dark clouds over us."

Simon was Kate's six-year-old cousin. With Tim in prison and Grace deciding that raising kids when marrying a man half her age didn't sound fun anymore, Simon was left with his seventy-year-old grandparents who didn't have the energy to raise a child.

"Didn't Simon's grandparents say they wouldn't fight you for custody?"

"Yeah, and they aren't, but it's Tim who refuses to sign over his parental rights and it's creating problems." I could hear the exasperation in her voice. "We get to see him a lot, I just want this mess wrapped up so he can feel secure again—in a home, with me and Adam."

"Makes sense. And you're an amazing person, Kate. I know things will work out. I just want you to have something happy to look forward to and plan for."

"I will. Just be ready, because the second we do set a wedding date you and Emma better be on a plane over here, Miss Maid of Honor."

"Of course!"

"So, how are things with you? I haven't seen you in months. Is your job going well?"

An uneasy laugh gurgled its way out. "The job is good." I hated lying, which was why I tried never to do it. Technically, I had stated the truth, but omitted details.

I glanced at the medical records in the manila envelope on the seat next to me. This was yet another situation I had to keep from Kate. The fact didn't sit well, but if anyone knew about this, it would be bad. Really, really bad and likely end before it began. Also, legally I couldn't talk about it. I had already signed a contract about keeping my mouth shut.

"Is your dad doing okay?" Kate asked.

I hung my head a little. "Not really. I talked to him a couple days ago. He, ah…well, I don't think he realized who I was."

"Oh, I'm so sorry, Meg."

"Yeah, me too." I fought back the tears. "But the doctor thinks that we might be able to slow down the memory loss if we start treatment soon and up his home care."

I wish I could quit my job and go back home, help my mother care for him, but then there would be no money coming in. Not the kind of money I was making at the hotel. And my father needed a medical professional, which was another thing I couldn't afford.

But that was going to change soon.

There were worse things than being married to a billionaire hotel heir. A billionaire hotel heir who was sexy and smart and made my body hum. The only difficult part, the part that made my stomach pinch, was the secrecy. How could I lie to Kate, my parents, Emma and the rest?

Easy. For my dad I could do anything.

I was getting married. I tossed those words around in my mind and—nope. Couldn't say it out loud. Not yet. I needed more time to let this sink in.

The car pulled up to the hotel.

"Hey, I just got to work, but I'll call you tomorrow, Kate."

"Okay. Love you, Meg. Call me anytime. For anything okay?"

"Okay. Love you too."

I clicked the phone off, snatched up the manila folder, and thanked the driver. It was dark and the spring air was crisp. I stopped at the lobby desk. Olivia was filling in tonight. A shift I should be working.

"Hi, Olivia, I'm sorry about the short notice."

"It's no trouble." Olivia was maybe a year younger than me and a part-timer. She filled in when people got sick or had appointments. She leaned over the desk. "I heard you're getting married to John Preston Strauss. Congratulations!"

"Thanks," I mumbled.

It was odd that this didn't seem odd to her. Maybe it was just me. Maybe to the outside world this was normal. Of course, there were bound to be people thinking the worst. Sleeping my way to the top and all that. Funny thing, one night of "sleeping" and I found myself in a situation I never saw coming.

"Mr. Strauss actually called me himself. Said he'd be staying in the penthouse for a couple months and I'd be filling in for you for a while."

"Oh, he did?"

She nodded spastically. "Which works out great for me because I could use the hours."

"That's good." I smiled because the girl had no idea what was going on and was obviously excited about working. "Have a good evening."

"Thanks, you too!"

I walked to the elevator, rode up, and headed to the penthouse. All day I had thought out this contract and what Preston wanted from me, but never once did I think of a counter stipulation of my own. Seeing Olivia working my shift slapped me with perspective. Three years was a long time of security, but I had to make sure I had something to go back to after my fake marriage to Preston Strauss ended.

Facing the penthouse door, I knocked. When no one answered, I pounded harder.

"Hello there." I spun around to see Preston standing in the office doorway across the hall. Tension racked my body as I marched toward him.

"Tough day, sweetheart?" He grinned.

"Other than realizing you gave my job away?" I pointed the folder at him.

"Did not." He snatched it out of my hand, turned and walked into the office flipping through it. I followed him.

"Then why did Olivia tell me you called her and said I'd be out for a while?"

"Everything looks good," he said going over my records and completely ignoring my question. "You're on the pill..." He flipped another page.

"Yeah, I have been for a while. You never said anything about giving my job to someone else."

"It's temporary." He snapped the folder shut and tossed it on the desk next to a small stack of papers. "With the wedding right around the corner, I figured you'd be busy with the planning and hosting guests...like your parents."

The way he annunciated the last word made me think he knew about more about my family than I thought.

I swallowed hard. "When exactly are we getting married?"

"I was thinking the sooner the better. Six weeks or so."

"Six weeks!"

"I thought you'd like it that way." His voice was soft and he folded his arms over his chest—not in a display of dominance but as if trying to determine exactly how to speak next. His cuffs were rolled at the sleeves and his jaw held that amazing shadow of a day's worth of stubble. Like the night I met him. He was sinful looking. Delicious. But when a sliver of sweet kindness trickled out, he was simply lethal.

I hadn't thought much of the details, what with just getting used to this charade in the first place. Somewhere deep down, I wanted a wedding soon too. My father grew worse every day and hopefully he'd remember who I was by the time he walked me down the aisle. It seemed silly wanting something like that, given everything going on with his health. But fake wedding or not, I desperately wanted my father there. I wanted him as mentally with me as he could be, but that was not something I wanted to discuss at the moment.

"I have a request regarding my job," I said.

He eyed me. "Oh?"

"After this marriage is done, I want my same job back, same pay, at the Chicago hotel."

He looked at me like I had asked him to name all fifty states in alphabetical order. "Are you mad about something?"

"Well, no, I guess I am just thrown that you would make a decision that affects my life without talking to me."

"That wasn't my intent, I just assumed that you'd be busy planning the wedding and could use the time. Plus, as my wife you won't need the money."

"This isn't about the money, I love my job and I love what I do. And I get that we aren't the normal, soon-to-be-married couple, but if we are going to make this work we need to talk to each other."

"I agree." He grinned and ran that hot gaze over my face, his smile widening to mega-watt status.

"Is something funny?"

He shook his head. "I'm sorry, it's just that most women wouldn't want to work if they didn't have to."

"I'm not like the women you know then."

"No," he looked at me and something in his eyes softened. "You aren't, are you? I will tell Olivia you are coming back full time and I will make sure there is a position for you in Chicago when the time comes."

"Thank you, that means a lot. But with the wedding being so close, maybe you're right and I should let Olivia fill in for a few weeks." I didn't want Olivia to lose out on the hours she seemed to need.

"I'll let her know," Preston said. Leaning forward, his voice lowered. "I don't know about you, but I think for our first pre-marital fight we did quite well."

Breath left my lungs. I hadn't realized I was holding it, and I laughed. The way his eyes sparkled with that boyish playfulness was too much to take in. The man was just gorgeous.

"Now, if you'll come sign these, we can get all this squared away." He gestured to the small stack of paper on the desk and I stepped toward him.

The contract.

He handed me a pen and explained every page as we went through it, always asking if I had questions. It was actually pretty thoughtful considering the circumstances.

When we got to the last page, I looked up at him.

"Last one." He smiled and trailed his fingertip along my chin. The gesture made me all gooey inside. Between the craziness of the situation, adrenaline crashing, and Preston's hands on me, it was almost like a calm, lust-induced mental state. Sign, sign, done.

No love.

No strings.

Just a business deal.

"This is for you." He reached into his pants pocket, pulled out a small black box, and set it on top of the contract. The inscription on the top read Harry Winston.

My hands shook as I opened it.

Oh. My. God. The center gem put that necklace from *Titanic* to shame. A princess cut blue diamond with small white diamonds surrounding it. It was beyond beautiful.

Tears filled my eyes. Not with joy. With sadness. This wasn't how I thought this day would be. A casual, "Here," and the signing of papers was not the romantic proposal I had dreamed about. Granted, the only comparison I had was my parents' story. They were at a carnival, Elvis was playing over the speakers, when my dad pulled my mom into his arms and swayed in the middle of the crowd. There, between cotton candy and "Can't Help Falling In Love With You," he placed a simple diamond on her finger.

"Say something," Preston whispered.

I shook my head. "I just thought this moment would involve more dancing," I muttered. Preston frowned, my last statement obviously making no sense.

"I mean…" Staring back at the ring, I tried to come up with something other than what was really going on in my head. "I didn't know diamonds came in this blue color."

The thing looked more like a gorgeous meteor than a piece of jewelry. It was the most incredible thing I'd ever seen.

"Don't you like it?"

"It's lovely," I said, recalling his words to me the night we met. I hadn't meant to sound so defeated or bratty, but it was the lackluster word that hit home. Everything should be fine. I should feel lucky, but I felt so…empty. So tired. And so alone.

The only person who knew what was really going on, with my parents and the money and all the mess of my past was Preston, and he offered me a nice cold diamond when all I wanted in that moment was something warm.

He maneuvered me to stand before him. My lower back pressed into the edge of the desk behind me and Preston cupped my face, forcing me to look up at him. His eyes were so unnerving. So expressive, yet so closed off.

"You make no sense," he whispered. I let out a half laugh half sob. "I thought women liked diamonds but you look truly miserable. Should I have taken you to Jared's?"

That time I really laughed. How did he do it? Make me feel better and comfortable while signing the next three years of my life away. I shook my head. "I'm not miserable. I just...I don't know what's real anymore."

He moved closer, his hips pressing against my stomach and the edge of the desk dug a little into the small of my back.

"This," he ran his thumb along my lower lip and my mouth parted, "is real."

Somehow that small sentiment ricocheted a plethora of fireworks though my bloodstream. His mouth came down on mine. He didn't move his thumb. Instead he pressed the pad inside my mouth and pushed down, opening my mouth wider. He delved his tongue inside and possessed everything I was in one long stroke.

I groaned and kissed him back. My mind was a ball of buzzing confusion, tension and excitement. I needed something, but I couldn't explain what. I just felt empty. And Preston was right there to hold me.

Just like a few nights ago, with a simple encounter, flash of a smile, and blunt words, he stoked the fire that was burning in me. A fire that I thought had been completely extinguished. All the tension from the last several hours, days, months, washed away. He didn't allow me to think about a thing. Feel a thing. All I could concentrate on was him. Surrounding me. Drinking me down.

His hands landed heavy on my ass. "You have," he trailed his lips down my neck, "the most amazing body."

He knelt before me and buried his face between my breasts, biting at the buttons of my shirt. His hands stayed firmly planted on my backside silently refusing to let go.

"Get this off," he growled. I instantly worked open my shirt and shrugged it off.

"Now this." He nipped at the lacy cup of my bra and I jumped because he snagged my nipple with it. The bite shot a zing of sensation to every limb. I reached around and unclasped the back and the scrap of fabric dropped to the floor.

He took one nipple into his mouth and sucked while his fingers dug into my ass cheeks. Yanking me closer to him. I moaned and arched my back.

"Fuck, you are a prize, Megan."

He kissed and nipped around my entire breast as if worshiping me. Like he had to touch every inch of my skin. I knew why I had fallen for this man once. Knew why I was falling again. Because he wasn't a man. He was a force. And I couldn't pull away. I didn't want to.

I fumbled around with his shirt and finally got it undone and off. His shoulders were hard and his skin the prettiest light mocha color. Flawless and smooth like freshly cooled taffy. Dark chocolate hair completed the edible essence of Preston Strauss.

My fingers wove into his thick hair and I kissed the top of his head. He trailed his lips lower, licking and kissing my ribs, down to my bellybutton and across my hip bone. I stood there dazed while a powerful, successful, incredibly sexy man was on his knees exploring me with his mouth.

I barely noticed him take my skirt down my legs.

"You know what two things I've been thinking of all day?"

I shook my head. "What?"

"If you were wearing those stockings again." His palms slid up my bare legs. "I liked them. But I love seeing all of you."

I had nothing to hide and even if I did, he'd find out. There was a liberation in the truth. A freedom in finally having someone else know everything.

Maybe he was right, maybe this was how smart adults mapped out what they wanted in a relationship. Because nothing in that moment felt clinical.

His hands trailed higher and my breath caught. "W-what was the other thing you've been thinking about?"

He smiled up at me. "What color panties you were wearing of course."

Passion radiated between us like a furnace and I gave myself up to it. He pulled down my panties, gently urging my legs apart as he went so that the elastic stretched taut against my thighs.

"Gorgeous. You know blue is my favorite color," he breathed and peeled them the rest of the way off. His breath hit my aching core. I was hot, shaky and so ready for him.

Reaching around, he palmed my ass and, as he rose to his feet, lifted me with him. Startled, but not surprised by his strength, I slapped my hands on his shoulders for balance and wound my legs around his hips.

He set me down on the desk with a thump, my bare ass atop the papers I had just signed. He kissed me hard and yanked his belt and pants open. I drove my tongue into his mouth, tasting all his masculine sweetness. All the power and intensity. His hard cock prodded at my entrance and I squirmed to get it into position. His arms were like a vice around me and he gripped the back of knees and pulled me into him.

His cock jammed into me and I cried out in pleasure.

"God, I've been wanting this, wanting you, all damn day." He withdrew and returned with an even harder thrust, bouncing my breasts and rustling the papers beneath me.

I placed my hands behind me for balance, causing my back to arch. He latched onto one aching nipple and sucked hard.

"Yes! Oh, Preston, more."

I had started the day in a very different mindset and was now in over my head for Preston. He fucked me impossibly hard. His hips banged against my inner thighs—that was going to leave a bruise—and the thought made my core clench.

"I feel you squeezing me," he growled. He gripped my lower back and yanked me into him.

"So deep…" I sobbed.

He hit a spot inside that sent a snap of bone-cracking pleasure surging through my entire body. Scoring my nails down his back, I held on and cried out for more.

My ass slipped along the papers, which were now scrunched and scattered across the desk. With every touch, every taste, every sound, I felt the connection between us. This was more than sex, this was a message. A promise.

He was taking me over. Branding me from the inside out. Every breath I took in his presence, every move in his direction, it was all woven together. Designed to make me lose control and surrender to him.

He had a contract that guaranteed no strings, but there he was, pulling mine.

And I let him.

Wanted him to.

"Come on, sweetheart," he breathed against my mouth. He wrapped an arm around my back and cupped my neck with the other. "I want to feel you come for me."

My skin was burning and my lungs overheating. I couldn't breathe, couldn't think. The pleasure was too much. It tingled in my toes until it felt as though my legs were on fire. He effortlessly hit that sensitive spot inside over and over, arching his hips just right at the end to rub his pelvis along my throbbing clit.

"I…I…Preston!" I hugged him close as my orgasm splashed through every cell like a molten tidal wave.

"That's it." He kissed my neck. "Come all over me."

Helpless against the raging wildness and searing white hot flash of pleasure, I had no choice but to obey and give in.

He whispered my name and his cock hardened further inside of me. The jolt from the engorgement and added pressure spurred another orgasm through me that blistered all the way to my bones.

His seed rushed into me and the warmth and intensity made me shudder. "I love feeling you…no barriers," he grated.

We were joined. In this moment, this feeling of passion and truth, the world seemed simple.

Breathing hard, I shifted slightly and the papers I was sitting on crumpled further. We both looked down at the mess we had made of the contract.

He tucked a lock of hair behind my ear and smiled.

"Well, I don't think we'll need a notary after all."

7

The sound of the shower turning off made me open my eyes and look around. Lying in bed, I could see the bathroom door was ajar. There were some ruffling sounds, then wet footsteps slapping the tile floor.

"Good morning," Preston said, strutting from the bathroom rubbing a towel over his head in nothing but a pair of black boxer briefs.

Good morning indeed. The man was beautiful. Tall, strong, so much cut muscle wrapped in tan skin. I wished Christmas to come early just to open such a nice package. Every time he moved his arm to run the towel along his brow, drying his hair, his bicep and abs flexed.

"You hungry?" he asked. My gaze snapped up to his.

"Huh?"

He lifted his chin slightly and unleashed all those straight pearly whites on me in a devious smile. "Must be. You're drooling."

When I slapped my palm over my mouth and clamped my lips together the smallest chuckle came from him. He walked over to the bed and I sat up, pulling the sheets to cover my breasts.

We had had an amazing night. It started in the office on the other end of the hall, but after mind-numbing pleasure, I vaguely remembered Preston carrying me back to the bedroom.

"What time is it?"

"Just after six."

Holy crap, no wonder I felt like my body had been hit by a truck, rather, Preston Strauss. I must have passed out sometime around midnight and didn't get my eight hours.

Stifling a groan was harder than I thought because one escaped my mouth.

"Someone's not a morning person." He smiled again.

I could get used to that sight, especially when it was pointed at me. It also made it hard to be grouchy when a nearly naked sex-god of a man was staring me down. Of course, I felt less than pretty at the moment, with bed-rumpled hair and mascara likely streaking down my face.

"Not all of us are machines," I called after him when he walked into the other room. Well, it was a closet, but it was big enough to be an actual living space.

"Food will be sent up soon and I made an appointment for you to meet with Jill Castor, the wedding planner, at three." He walked out of the closet, wearing steel-gray pants and black belt and buttoning up a white collared shirt. "Before that you should go to your apartment and get some of your things."

I bunched the sheets tighter against my sternum. "My stuff? And bring it here?"

"You are my fiancé, so yes, living with me would be required."

"But, it's a hotel."

He looked at his wrist and buttoned the cuffs. "I travel a lot, but I'll purchase a suitable house after a wedding."

I knew my mouth was hanging open again, but for a whole different reason this time. This shouldn't be a shock, yet it was. Yes, there was the contract and yes we poured over the technicalities mercilessly, but all the details that accompanied moving in with someone flooded to my brain.

"There are a lot of matters to consider but we'll take it in steps," he said, straightening and looking sinful in his casual take on the standard suit. His shirt was tucked in, but unbuttoned at the top, and his lean hips lined with that ash fabric lined his body perfectly. Must have been tailored because it fit him like a dream.

"I like my apartment though." The thought of having some-place to run to—just in case—made me feel a tad better about this whole situation.

"You can keep it. You won't need to bring furnishings here obviously. Just some clothes and comforts you'd like. The rest will be taken care of."

"But…" I ran a hand through my hair.

He frowned like he had last night when he gave me the ring, which was on the bedside table. I didn't have the nerve to put it on yet.

"What?"

"This is just…weird."

One moment we were signing a contract and going over legalities, then we had a night with a few perfect moments where things felt real—like we really were a couple and had a legitimate connection. Now it was back to the sterile lists of tasks and chores, as if last night hadn't happened. The distance, the professionalism, was in place and I felt more like an employee with a to-do list than a fiancé.

"It will take time to adjust." His tone was quick, but not harsh. Speaking another inevitable truth about the situation we were in.

I nodded because he was right. I had made the choice. He didn't force me. And I had reasons, good reasons, for agreeing. But getting my feelings and emotions under control and onboard was proving to be a difficult task, especially when I was starting to feel something real for Preston. I didn't know what I felt, or how seri-ous it was, but it was there and I was afraid it was going to grow until it complicated things.

He came to the bedside table, grabbed his watch, and fastened it. Leaning down, he kissed me quickly on the top of my head.

"I have several late meetings tonight, but I'll have a credit card, personal bank card and a list of necessary phone numbers delivered later on today," he stated, and walked out of the bedroom.

When I heard the front door open and close, I knew he was gone. The sheets were cold and I sat there confused and a little sad, which was stupid. I had gotten myself into this. This was a contract with no complications or overblown emotions.

It was time I started understanding that.

I walked up the steps to my apartment and unlocked it. Everything was clean and sparse. Emma had texted me yesterday saying she would be out of town for work for the next couple days. She kept her own schedule and traveled a fair amount for various clients and projects. While I missed her, I found myself kind of relieved she wasn't home at the moment.

She was my only real friend in New York and aside from Kate, the best one I'd ever had. But I couldn't bring myself to tell anyone about the Preston situation yet. I couldn't tell them about the contract, which meant despite all my "good reasons," I'd be lying to everyone when I broke the news that I was engaged.

I walked through my room, stuffing clothes into my suitcase, then got all my toiletries from the bathroom. My forehead was hot and my head was pounding. I used to get "stress-sick" back when I was in college. Low-grade fevers and achiness. Splashing some cool water on my face, I looked up and caught my reflection in the mirror and I practiced my "happily-ever-after face."

"So I spoke with Preston earlier and he said you wanted the wedding at his hotel."

Jill Castor was the best wedding planner in New York City, and every other city for that matter. She planned events for the wealthy and famous, and Preston was insistent that she plan ours.

We sat at The Strauss Hotel Bar. She sipped her cranberry juice and I just stared at my Diet Coke, which I hadn't touched. My head was pounding and I could tell that I was still running a fever. "Fabulous choice, and convenient," she said, flipping through a massive portfolio.

Attempting to ignore the throbbing pain radiating from my ear to my skull, a clear sign that I had a full-blown ear infection, I focused on Jill. Her tight gray bun was fastened to the top of her head and her brown eyes had a nice quality. She had to be in her early fifties, and she was petite and dressed in a cream pantsuit with a chunky gold necklace lining her throat.

"You know it can take years, if ever, to get on the list to have a wedding at The Strauss Hotel."

"Yeah well, that's what sleeping with the boss will get you— bumped up the list."

She laughed and I took a sip of my drink. It was funny because it was true.

"Either way, it will be beautiful. Now, I have a lot of ideas. I think that we should tackle the engagement party first since you two are moving right along. I think Friday the fifteenth for the party then have the wedding Saturday evening. We'll block off a few floors of rooms for your guests, and have a two-day celebration. A celebrity couple did it and it was fabulous. However, we won't be outside." She shuddered a little bit and her thin mouth turned down with distaste when uttering the word "outside."

"Okay." My quick response seemed to surprise her. If only she knew I was bound to be the easiest fake bride in the world to please. Plus, her idea made the most sense. My dad wouldn't do well traveling once to New York for an engagement party then back a few weeks later for the wedding.

"I'll take care of the announcement in the *Times* and the *Post*." She flipped to another page. "Now," she folded her hands and looked at me, "tell me what you're thinking."

"I was actually thinking this should be spiked." I jiggled my glass of Diet Coke.

She smiled. "No, I mean, what do you want for your wedding?"

"Um…" I looked down. "I guess I haven't really thought about it. It's all happened so fast."

"Oh, sweetie, every girl has thought about it. Tell me that vision you have. The one you've been dreaming about since you were little. I find that if I can get to the root of my client's childhood fantasy, it gives me a sense of your expectations and makes for smooth sailing."

Her words sunk in and I recalled the days when I used to be optimistic about love and the future. I guess I had thought about it a long time ago. Not in so much detail. I focused more on the idea of being in love and walking down the aisle seeing "the one" for the first time. In my dream I had been ridiculously in love, my parents were stable and my father was mentally healthy. Everyone was just…

"Happy," I whispered.

"What, sweetie? I didn't hear you?" Jill leaned over the table slightly.

I straightened my shoulders and looked at her. "I guess I've always wanted to just be happy."

She nodded. "And do you see that in more of a ball gown or mermaid dress?"

I smiled. How did you put a feeling into a dress? "I guess more simple. Elegant."

She nodded and pulled out another book. Running her eyes over me, she licked her fingers and began spastically flipping through the book.

"You're tall, lean with some shape," she paused to wink at me, "Ah, here! Look at this."

She placed the book of dresses before me, opened to the middle. I about lost my breath. It was the most beautiful dress I'd ever seen. Strapless and fitted with just a slight feathering flare past the hips that made it look like it had tiny pieces of clouds woven into it. A tear stung my eye.

"Well, I'd say that's a good start." She patted my hand. "Now call up your girls and go dress shopping. But if this is close to what you have in mind, I can build the wedding theme around that."

I nodded and ran a fingertip under my eye.

"I'm sorry, this is silly. I don't know why I'm so emotional."

"Oh sweetie, I love working with first-time brides, everything is still so magical."

I laughed a little because I could see how wedding number three may not be as romantic as the first. As I sat there, getting questions fired at me about my dream wedding, I realized that the little hollow part in my stomach started feeling a little less...hollow. Not because of the wedding or money or even the planning. But because every time I thought about what would come two months from now, I thought of Preston. Thought of him standing at the altar. Thought of me walking toward him. And that made my heart pound a little faster and my skin heat, which, despite my fever, would have been a good thing.

Jill pulled out a color palette. "Now, let's talk about accent colors."

● ● ●

"I brought Chinese food," Preston said, coming through the door. He set it down on the coffee table and looked at me balled up on the couch. "What's the matter?"

"Not feeling so great."

He frowned. "Why didn't you call?"

Lifting my head from the armrest, I clutched the afghan tighter. "You were working. There's nothing you can really do—"

The back of his fingers gently brushed over my brow before I could finish my sentence.

"You have a fever." He walked into the kitchen. After rustling with what sounded like pills, and the faucet turning on and off, he came back with Tylenol and a glass of water.

"It's an ear infection. I use to get them before finals a lot."

He handed me the pills and water. I took them.

"I'll call the physician and see if I can get you in tomorrow."

I nodded. "Thank you."

"You hungry?"

"Not really."

He sat on the couch next to me. Gently grabbing my shins, he placed my feet in his lap and pressed his thumbs into my instep, slowly moving up. I closed my eyes and fought the urge to moan in bliss.

"Megan," press, "You said for this to work we had to work together. That goes both ways. So don't keep things from me." His tone was rough and something in his eyes flickered with a mixture of pain and anger. "If you're feeling sick, you have to tell me. I can help you before it gets unmanageable. Understand?"

My throat closed up a bit and something very raw, very dark, masked Preston's charming features.

"Okay," I whispered.

He nodded and leaned back a little. "Good. Now get comfortable, because next up are your shoulders."

8

"Hi, Daddy," I said and clutched the phone to my ear.

"Meg-Pie!"

My heart was about to burst with relief. When my phone rang, I expected it to be the wedding planner. Jill had called on average four times a day since I met with her last week. It was fun planning a wedding, but exhausting. Clutching my small grocery bag, I walked from the store back to the hotel up the street.

"How you doing, kiddo?"

"I'm good, dad. Just running some errands."

"Errands? Shouldn't you be home in bed?" His voice grew concerned. "Mom said you were sick."

"It was just an ear infection," I explained, leaving out that it had been a bad one. And one hundred percent stress-induced. "The doctor told me to take it easy for a few days." Which I did, with Preston right by my side the entire time. He had been so normal and sweet, like a real fiancé. Taking me to the doctor, filling my prescription and making sure I ate. But something about me being sick obviously unnerved him. As if he needed to heal me himself. Still, his attentiveness and world-class foot rubs had me pushing the edge of spoiled. "How are you doing, Dad?"

"Oh, pretty good. Wish your mother would stop fussing over me all the time."

"Ah, she just loves you."

God, this was wonderful. It had been a long time since I had a conversation with my father like this. Like he was there...all the way present in the moment and lucid.

"The hotel business treating you well?" he asked.

I smiled. If only he knew just how well. "It is."

"Anyone special in your life?"

I swallowed and the spring breeze hit my face as I walked a bit faster. Now was a perfect time to tell him. Tell him that Preston and I were getting married. I opened my mouth to try, but no words came out.

"Megan," he chided. "You work too hard. You need to take time for yourself."

"I know, Dad. I just, I'm pretty busy. But I have a few friends at work and having Emma here has been great."

"Well, that's good. I just don't want you to shy away from the other stuff. What that prick did is unforgivable."

"Daddy, I'm so sorry about Tim and the money—"

"Tim? Forget that low-life. I'm talking about Brian. He's the real loser. No one hurts my baby girl like he did. He'll get his, Meg-Pie. You just take care of you and don't be afraid to get out there. You're a treasure, honey."

If I wasn't juggling groceries in one hand and my cell in the other, I would have wiped the tears lining my eyes.

"Thanks, Daddy."

"You don't be a stranger okay? I haven't talked to you in weeks."

Now the tears stung for a different reason. I talked to my father at least twice a week, this was just the first time he called me and knew who I was.

"Okay, Dad. I love you."

"Love you too, Meg-Pie."

He hung up and something deep in my chest ached. I didn't know when I'd hear him talk to me like that again. What if he never did? What if that was last time my father had a "good day?"

Reaching the entrance to The Strauss Hotel, I realized why I hadn't told him about Preston. Told him while he could understand. Because I didn't want one of the best conversations, maybe the last one in which he knew who I was, to be tainted with a lie.

I was marrying Preston. But when my father asked me if I loved him, and he would have, I would have had to say yes. Living a false reality was one thing. Admitting it out loud was another. But lying to my father?

Never.

● ● ●

"What's all this?" Preston asked as he entered the kitchen of the penthouse.

"Just got a few groceries. I was going to make dinner tonight." When I lifted to my tip toes to put away the noodles in a high cabinet, causing my shirt to ride up, Preston's fingers skated along the exposed small of my back.

"I was unaware you were so domestic." His breath danced along the back of my neck as his palm trailed around my side, resting low on my stomach.

Over the last week, I'd learned that his warmth was addicting. Okay, so I knew that after the first night. But now, my body was recognizing his as a mandatory essence. A fix I needed. When he was near, I didn't feel so overwhelmed. So alone.

"You feeling better?"

His concern made my heart flutter a little. "Yes. Almost done with the round of antibiotics and I haven't had a fever in days."

"I'm glad." His lips brushed against my ear and a flash of lust roiled through my bones and spread to every surface of my skin.

I turned to face him. His green eyes were like getting lost in Oz and for a moment, I forgot about cooking and just wanted to wrap myself around him.

"I recognize that look," he growled and leaned in to nip my earlobe. "And while I'd love nothing more than to fuck you right here on the counter, we have to get going."

I frowned up at him. Mostly because he just painted an exciting picture in my mind only to snatch it away. "Where are we going?"

"The Park Avenue Armory. Striker Solutions is having a gathering."

I'd heard of Striker. It was the company that handled all of the security for The Strauss Hotel. They provided personal drivers who were really bodyguards, and closets that doubled as panic rooms. This company employed some of the top security detail money could buy.

"Looking to change career paths?" I smiled.

"Rhys Striker is the founder of the company. He's a good friend and tonight is his annual Chairman's Ball. Since I am one of his original clients and investors, I'm expected to attend. And," he leaned in and tugged at my lower lip with his teeth, "since you are my fiancé everyone is expecting to see you on my arm. Although right now the only place I want to see you is naked and on me."

I wrapped my arms around his neck and pulled so our bodies were pressed together. "How about naked on the counter?"

My mouth met his, delivering a dozen languid, yet hungry kisses before he pulled back with a frustrated growl.

He rested his forehead against mine. Both of us were breathing heavily. It took me a moment to realize that I was no longer standing on the floor, but my feet dangled off the counter and Preston stood between my thighs. Hard and ready.

"I need you to remember exactly where we are right now, how your hands are pulling my hair, how your eyes are begging me to fuck you, how your pussy is wet with want, because the second we get home tonight I am going to flip you against this counter and show you exactly where I want you."

He took a step back and ran a hand though his thoroughly mussed hair. "Now, get moving and try on something from the closet I stocked for you last week."

"I take it this is a fancy kind of thing."

"It is."

I smiled. And it felt forced and hurt a little. If I were being honest, I'd admit to the disappointment spreading through me. My plan for tonight, my world-class lasagna, a cable movie and pajamas-optional activity, was a no-go. It had been a long day. The good part had a cloud hanging over it. Hearing my father's voice free of confusion was darkened by refraining, once again, from telling someone important in my life what was really going on.

I just needed a night of normalcy and calm. But like most things, my expectations needed to change. Preston's life didn't allow for a lot of snuggle time.

"Contract stipulates I accompany you to events so I'll just go get ready." I'd meant for that to sound playful, but it came out more sad than anything. Scooting around Preston, I made my way toward the bedroom closet. I started looking through the dresses on the hangers.

Preston stood in the door jamb, his forearms resting on the sides of the entry. "I'll introduce you to a lot of people, but I'll likely be tied up in conversations for most of the evening."

"Okay," I said, gently flicking through the clothes my eyes never meeting his.

"Maybe you'd like to invite Emma? May make you feel a bit more comfortable."

I stopped mid-swipe at the latest Chanel number and looked at him. He was trying. I could see it on his face that he was attempting to genuinely make me happy.

"I would like that."

A big smile splayed across his face like he'd just answered the right question to final *Jeopardy*. My chest instantly split open with the joy of seeing such an incredible man that elated.

A small laugh escaped because I had seen this kind of thing with my parents. My father was crazy about my mom. Every time she smiled, he got this goofy grin of pure bliss as if his whole life was wrapped around making this one woman truly happy.

But that smile…it made my heart race. Right now it was a gala. Tomorrow it would be something else. It would mostly likely never be a couch, junk food and sweatpants night. No matter what though, it was limited and conditional. Two words I needed to get acquainted with quickly.

● ● ●

"Great balls of Christ this place is insane!" Emma whispered in my ear as we walked into the Amory. The historic building was all red brick and simply beautiful. The inside main area could have been used for anything, from a concert to a car show, but tonight, it was decked out with silk laid tables and candles. A shiny wooden dance floor led to a large stage where the orchestra played.

"I thought you said you've been to these sort of things before?" I whispered back.

"Yeah, a few of Adam's stuffy charities and parties but this is still…" she shook her head and I knew what she meant.

Overwhelming.

Tuxedos and ball gowns, and circling servers holding silver trays of finger food, littered the entire area. Emma lifted her chin in the air like she belonged there, and I followed suit. The wealthy and rich surroundings never really shocked me before, but this was on another level. Still, as far as these people knew, I was supposed to be there. Now if only I actually felt that way.

"I knew you were dating the boss but damn," Emma whistled low. "By the way, I am totally happy I finally got to meet him. I can see why you put out so quick."

"About that..." She turned and faced me, her short purple dress flowing around her hips. Though she was petite, Emma had a natural beauty most women would kill for. "Preston and I are sort of, more than dating."

"What does that mean?"

"We're getting—"

Crap! That last word lodged in my throat like a sour Skittle I couldn't spit out. Taking a deep breath, I reminded myself why this was happening—why I had agreed to this scam and *why* I needed to pull myself together and own it. People won't believe we're a happy couple if the bride-to-be looks unpleasant all the time.

"Preston proposed. We're getting married."

I tried to do that excited and happy face, but Emma stared at me like I was having a Tourette's meltdown.

"Ladies," Preston said, holding two flutes of champagne out. We took them.

"Thank you," I said a little softer than I meant.

"Are you ready?" he asked quietly.

I nodded.

"Hold up, you two are getting married?" One dainty hand around her drink, Emma pointed at Preston.

"Yes. We are," Preston said.

Emma let out a long breath. She was never one to pry or judge. In fact, she was more easygoing than most men, but her brows furrowed tightly, like she couldn't decide what to say next.

Finally, she looked at me. "Is this what you want?"

The question hit me like one of Emma's famously bragged about bitch-slaps. I didn't know exactly what to expect her reaction to be, so the only thing I could do was stick to the truth the best I could.

I looked at Preston and smiled, then back at Emma. With all the confidence in the world on my side I said, "Marrying Preston is definitely something I want."

"Okay then." Emma held up her flute. "I'm happy for you guy."

"Thank you," Preston said.

She leaned in and whispered something low to him. I couldn't make out exactly what, but something along the lines of, "hurt her," and "balls torn off," were key words I picked up on. Preston smiled and nodded.

"I understand."

"Great! Then we're good."

"Now if you ladies care to join me, I'd like to introduce you to a few people." Preston casually rested his palm on the small of my back. Since the first night I met him, he'd been guiding me through rooms. Gently coaxing me in the direction of his choosing—a fact that was not lost on me.

My powder blue dress barely grazed the floor as he led me toward a small crowd of people on the other side of the room. The silk was tight from my breasts to my hips then subtly flared out. Emma and I looked to be the only ones who wore our hair down instead of some intricate up-do. As if Preston could read my thoughts he leaned in and said, "I'm proud to have you on my arm."

We reached the group of older gentlemen, all looking like a cross between Bill Gates and the Monopoly guy. Except for one.

"Rhys, this is my fiancé Megan and our friend Emma Wade."

"I've heard a lot about you," Rhys said and shook my hand. The man was massive. Not quite as tall as Preston, but over six foot with the broadest shoulders I'd ever seen. His smoky gray eyes and longish blond hair made him look more like a superhero in a tux than a CEO of Striker Solutions.

"It's nice to meet you." I smiled, but his attention was already turned to Emma.

"Miss Wade," he said. If I hadn't known better, I would have thought Emma shuddered a little when he took her hand in his.

Preston and Rhys started talking business, a few details spilling out here and there. Rhys was a former Marine and moved as though he knew where everyone in the room was at any given time—a trait that likely made him very good at his job. But his gaze kept landing on Emma.

I stood there, sipping my champagne, perfectly happy to be listening and not talking. Emma, on the other hand, kept fidgeting and looking at Mr. Marine. I'd never seen her so affected by a man.

The orchestra slowed the beat and Rhys held out his hand to Emma. "Care to dance, Miss Wade?"

Emma put her empty champagne flute on a server tray passing by and nodded. Holy crap! Brassy, tough-talking Emma was speechless. Rhys led her to the dance floor among the other couples swaying. When she looked over her shoulder at me, I smiled wide.

"Preston." A middle-aged man approached and shook his hand. "Strauss Hotel is doing well. I hear John is retiring soon."

"We'll see," Preston replied. "David, this is my fiancé, Megan Riley."

More pleasantries, handshakes and fake smiles took up the next two hours. I hadn't said more than a few words to anyone, and most were just formal greetings. Over and over Preston was approached, confidently holding court in his own corner of the ballroom while the crowd came to him. And I was just another bird in that flock. Pulled in by that invisible power and charisma he radiated.

Emma was doing her own mingling, mostly with Rhys, and I stood, staring into space, trying to figure out what part of Preston was more enthralling—

"A-hundred-thousand for your thoughts?" Preston whispered into my ear.

I smiled at him. "Isn't it, 'a penny'?"

He shrugged. "I like to aim high."

"Well, that's quite a price for a single thought."

"Depends." He faced me fully, the crowd around us faded away and the heat of him engulfing me. "Tell me your thoughts were of me and I'll double my price." His green eyes shimmered like glossy emeralds and like usual, I was mesmerized.

"Would you like to dance?"

My heart pounded hard, and while this night hadn't gone as I had originally planned, there was nothing more I wanted to do in that moment than wrap myself in Preston's arms and let the world fade away.

"So much," I whispered.

Taking me by the hand, he led me to the center of the room and I realized that it could have been to the gates of hell, I still would have followed.

9

●●●●●●●

It was late. I didn't know exactly how late, but enough to where my body ached and my feet stung from being pinched in the high heels. I walked into the closet, stepped out of the strappy death traps and peeled off the dress. I was too tired to rummage for a nighty and honestly, I wasn't feeling sexy enough for any more silk and lace. Grabbing one of Preston's white tee-shirts off the shelf I pulled it on and walked out of the closet and into the bathroom to brush my teeth and wash my face.

"Did you have a nice time?" Preston called from the bedroom.

"The Armory was beautiful and Rhys seems nice." I needed to talk to Emma about how *nice* of time she had. She was quiet on the ride home and I didn't want to push for details in front of Preston, but it was obvious she seemed to connect with the security CEO.

"Rhys is a good friend," Preston called out again. This time it sounded like he was in the closet. It was funny how we seemed to move around each other so fluidly at times. "He'll be at the wedding."

Walking from the bathroom I pulled the comforter back on the bed. I glanced up to see Preston standing on the other side—

"Whoa," I breathed.

Sheets in my hand, I froze and simply stared. Preston in a pair of low slung gray pajama pants and nothing else. There was something so incredibly sexy about him, but this? Hard, tan torso muscles tapering to lean hips and that small trail of hair that started just below his navel and disappeared below his pants made my mouth water.

"I see you have the top to my bottoms," he grinned. I looked down the front of me. His shirt hit mid-thigh and I hadn't bothered to cover up further.

"Hope you don't mind?" I asked, hadn't thinking to do so before.

He shook his head. His expression was stern but other than that, he looked so relaxed, so normal, in slightly disheveled hair and five o'clock shadow. He slowly walked around the edge of the bed toward me, never taking his gaze from my face.

"This arrangement is different for me too, you know." His voice was low and those green eyes seared hot. My body responded in every way, recognizing that once again, I was the piece in his sights. Any feeling of exhaustion was gone, replaced with anticipation. My nipples hardened and the scratch of the soft cotton tee was enough to make me groan. "I don't stay the night with women." Step. "I don't play house." Step. "I *don't* share my clothes."

I swallowed hard. His gruff voice would have supported the idea of him being mad, but the hunger in his eyes, the way he shifted his body with every move toward me made me think he was after something very different. Me.

Rounding the corner of the bed, he closed in. "So explain to me why, standing in *my* shirt, next to *my* bed, in *my* penthouse, do I want you more than I have before?"

Breathing was proving more difficult the longer I stayed near Preston. There I stood, no makeup, tangled hair, and he made me feel more beautiful in that moment than the entire evening I stood by him in a designer gown.

"I don't know," I whispered.

He cupped my hips. Fisting the material, he slowly tugged the shirt up, exposing more of my thighs.

"Maybe things are different for you now." My voice trembled.

His eyes were fixed on the hem riding higher and higher. "No. *You* are different."

His mouth hovered over mine and the crisp smell of him engulfed me. Placing my palms on his hard stomach, I lifted to my toes and pressed my lips against his.

A small groan vibrated down my throat. I kissed him like I had been wanting to for the past five hours. Like I did the night we first met. Planning the wedding, running errands and adapting to the contractual life we'd set up melted away. It was just us. And we knew the truth. Wrapping my arms around him, I pulled him closer. Desperate to hang on to this moment. Hang on to him.

"Megan," he growled between laps at my mouth. His big body gently pushed against me and I fell back on the bed. He was over me in a heartbeat, kissing my neck. His warm hands slid up my thighs and gripped my panties, slowly trailing them down my legs and off.

Moving that amazing mouth lower, he bit at my nipple straining beneath the white cotton. I jolted from the delicious sting.

"We're going to keep this on," he said, tugging more of the shirt, and my breast, between his teeth. A sharp sizzle of lust coursed through my veins. "Because the next time I wear it, I want to picture you," he sucked hard on my other nipple, wetting the material covering it, "like this."

I gripped his shoulders, willing him to continue. Anything he wanted, I'd give him, so long as he just stayed with me. Stayed right there, holding me. Surrounding me with his warmth. His affection. I didn't care what that meant. Didn't care that this man had already consumed such a big part of me in a short amount of time. None of it mattered. Because he was more than anything I had ever experienced. Made me feel like I was beyond the person I was.

"Want you," I whispered. "More."

With his face buried between my breasts and delivering licks and nips of pleasure, I reached down and fumbled with his pants, finally working them off his legs and to the floor.

His hard cock pressed against my inner thigh and burned me like a hot steel rod. I needed him. Inside me. Part of me.

"Please Preston. Now." My voice was more like a sob, begging for the connection I had been missing from him.

"You're not ready." Fists on either side of my head, he rose up and kissed me hard. Delving his tongue deep in my mouth then retreating, mimicking what his intentions were. Gripping his wrist, I pulled his hand to my mouth and sucked his fingertips.

"Now."

He growled and took his newly wetted fingers, reached between our bodies and rubbed the head of his cock, moistening it.

"You drive me crazy," he grated, positioning himself at my entrance.

"Good," I whispered. Because he was taking over my mind completely.

He thrust hard, seating himself to the hilt in one stroke. I hissed a breath. It was a tight fit, but it felt so good. He felt good. Wrapping my legs around him, I cupped his face in my palms and kissed his chin, his nose, his cheeks. Wild and out of my mind for him, I just wanted to touch him, taste him everywhere.

He grabbed my wrists and yanked them over my head, pinning them into the mattress. He rocked in and out, his chest scraping against my breasts causing the barrier of the shirt to ride up. A surge of wetness rushed, making his cock slide easier within me. I was already on the brink.

"Not yet," he growled.

In one quick movement, he withdrew from me, rose to his knees and flipped me to my stomach. Lifting my hips, he positioned me so that I was on my hands and knees, my ass high in the air. He threw the hem of my shirt up so more of my bottom was exposed and gripped my hips.

"You're going to come when I'm deep inside you." He buried himself once more into my pussy.

"Oh, God!" My finger dug into the sheets.

Preston's strokes quickened. Pumping in and out, hitting that spot over and over. My inner walls clamped down on him, ready to erupt from the pleasure he was driving into me. He grabbed the back of my shirt and yanked me up. Never severing the connection, I straddled his thighs, my back against his chest, and gave myself up to his desires.

One strong arm wrapped around me, just below my breasts. He held me flush against him while his other hand came around to rub my aching clit. Heat surged and I was on the edge of losing myself. My body. My mind. All of it to him.

"Now," he nipped my earlobe, "you can come."

His hips shot up and plunged even deeper while his fingers worked the sensitive bundle of nerves in fast circles. I catapulted over the ledge so hard and fast that my vision went blurry and all my muscles tensed and relaxed over and over in a mind-blowing orgasm. My head fell back against his shoulder and I cried out his name as the pleasure continued. He didn't stop and I loved every slide and retreat of his thick cock.

His body hummed, his gripped tightened. He bit down on my neck and a low growl shot from his throat as he came inside me. Hot and heady. I felt whole. Warm and wanted from the inside out.

But when he didn't loosen his grip, just kept me close, I turned my head enough to kiss the base of his jaw. The last thing I heard was him murmuring my name and asking, "What have you done to me, Megan?"

10

I sank back into the water and closed my eyes. Resting my neck against the edge of the bathtub, I let the bubbles dance around me and soothe my skin. It had been a long day. Not particularly bad, but long.

The last week had been great. He worked a lot and while we only saw a bit of each other in the mornings and evenings, progress was being made. Everyday things seemed more real. Felt more real.

It was late and once again, Preston still wasn't back. I didn't know why I was tired lately. The list of things I had to do was growing daily, but my energy seemed to be lessening. Number one on the "to do" list was tell people I was engaged.

Emma was the only one who knew and I had asked her not to say anything to Adam or Kate until I could tell them. She hadn't. And besides a few text messages about how I'd better not make her wear an ugly bridesmaid's gown or carry a parasol down the aisle, she hadn't really pushed me on the details. Every time I had tried to ask her about Rhys, she avoided the topic. It looked like we both had our own private issues.

"What the hell are you doing?"

My eyes snapped open and I looked at Preston standing in the doorway, leering down at me. I'd never seen so much rage on someone's face.

I sat up and wrapped my arms around my breasts. "I'm taking a bath."

A muscle ticked in his jaw as he examined the obviousness of what I just said. His green eyes held so much bleak hate as he looked along the length of the tub, then at me.

"Get the fuck out."

He turned and stomped away. Stunned that he just spoke to me like that, I shot out of the bath, grabbed the robe on the back of the door and fastened it. Rushing to the bedroom, Preston stood by the mini bar, pouring himself a drink.

"What is your problem?" I demanded and swayed a bit on my feet. Between my body temperature quickly changing from a hot bath to cool air adding to my already dizzy exhaustion, standing was a bit tough.

He faced me, drink in hand. "I don't like you in the bathtub," he stated plainly, as if that should clear everything up.

"Yeah, caught that. But why?"

"Because." His glare was so strong I was worried just aiming that thing at someone could cause internal combustion. Something was obviously up with him, but there was no way he'd get away with speaking to me like that.

"I didn't sign up to be barked at, and I certainly didn't see a 'no bathtub' clause in the contract."

"Then I'll get that amended and have a fresh document for you to sign tomorrow," he snapped.

"No way." I crossed my arms. "I agreed to play by your rules but you can't go changing things on a whim. Especially stupid things like bathing and—"

"Yes. I can," he growled.

"No. You can't, Preston."

"And what are you going to do? Walk away?" He closed in on me and my heart sped up a bit. He was so imposing.

Preston wasn't the type of man to hurt a woman, if anything, he was more gentle in a lot of respects when it came to them, from what I'd been able to tell. But this was the first time his anger was directed at me. And I had no idea why.

"I can walk away, Preston. If we're going to start to play chicken with each other, see who will walk first on day two into this arrangement, then you need to seriously consider how badly you want this to work."

His nostrils flared. He knew I was calling him out and honestly, I hoped my nerve held up. Backing down now would make for a rough three years…if we even made it that far.

"There is a perfectly good shower. Don't take a bath again." His voice was deeper, rougher in a way I'd never heard. Normally he projected power and a kind of charisma that drew people in. This was different. Like wrath was swirling over him and something very dark was clawing at the surface.

"Why?"

"Because I'm asking." That time his voice held an edge of vulnerability.

I wanted to remind him that this whole situation was based on trust. Instinct told me that this was an issue and to push now would be a mistake. A big one. And a man like Preston didn't do a damn thing if he didn't want.

"Since you asked," I drew out the last word, "I won't take a bath again."

"Good." He nodded and stomped into the closet. I could hear him changing but he didn't say another word. I stood there wondering just how much of Preston would remain a mystery.

● ● ●

"It's dinner, not a sentencing," Preston said in my ear.

"I hope so, I didn't dress for death row." I tried to joke but my nerves were wired and going crazy. I was nervous. Actually, far, far beyond nervous.

"You look lovely," Preston said and steered me out of the town car and onto a busy sidewalk.

I was really starting to hate that word because he always said it with such indifference. He could have chosen a worse phrase though, I suppose. We hadn't said more than two words to each other in three days. Ever since that bathtub incident. If I'd known better, I'd think he had been either ignoring me or avoiding me.

Despite the distance between us, he had come to bed every night. Always sneaking in after I fell asleep and up before I woke. The only reason I knew he'd been there was because the sheets were still warm and his wonderful masculine smell still lingered on his pillow. It was odd, but a part of me was missing him.

We walked into a very nice, very expensive-looking restaurant in downtown Manhattan. The host led us to a private room where Preston's father, brother and another woman sat waiting. They all stood when we entered.

"Megan, my dear!" John came around the table and wrapped me in a hug. He was so warm and happy it calmed my nerves a bit. "You look radiant."

"Thank you, sir."

"Don't you dare," he scolded. "You call me John, or Dad."

His smile was so genuine it made my chest twist and think of my own father. Charlie cleared his throat and I turned to face him.

"Megan, you remember my brother Charlie, and this is his wife, Darlene."

Charlie nodded and Darlene looked me over with a smile plastered to her face that looked more Botox-induced than anything else. She was a bit shorter than I, but built like an exotic belly dancer. With dark eyes and hair, everything about her radiated confidence and money. I had never felt so weird around a woman. She gave off a vibe that I didn't really like but couldn't put my finger on why.

"She's adorable, Preston," Darlene said.

And then it hit. The reason I didn't like her. Something behind her eyes when she looked at Preston rubbed me wrong. There was an obvious history between them, and tension so thick I could cut it with a knife.

I grit my teeth and attempted to smile.

"Indeed," Preston said, and pulled out my chair.

I tried not to fuss with my light yellow lace dress. It was both pretty for spring and evening wear. I loved it because it made me feel feminine and sexy without being over the top. The men were all in suits and Darlene's tight red number was sleek, tight and left little to the imagination.

"I pre-ordered everything," John said to us when the waiter came in and poured everyone wine.

The room was low lit and the nearby candles flickered light off the white tablecloth. It was private and chic.

"I hope you don't mind." Charles looked at me and I shook my head. He was at the end of the table, Preston sat to his right and I next to him while Charlie and Darlene were across the table from us.

"Of course not." I smiled.

"Have you ever been here, Megan?" Darlene asked, taking a sip of her wine.

"No, I haven't."

"It does take a while for reservations typically. This place certainly isn't for everyone." She shrugged and I didn't miss the dig on my 'status,' thrown in there.

"How's the property in Beijing looking?" Charlie asked Preston.

"Are you really discussing business, Charlie? We're in the company of beautiful ladies." John winked at me.

"I agree," Preston said. His palm slid along the top of my thigh.

I looked over at him and a hungry green gaze met mine. An instant heat threaded through my veins. Damn it, I had been missing him. Even though our arrangement was only a few weeks old, I was accustomed to him. I pined for his attentions. One thing I was learning was that when things were good, they were so good. I wanted that heat. Wanted him to look at me, make me fall the way he did that first night, and every night after when his skin was against mine.

"How did you two meet?" Darlene piped in, interrupting our silent moment.

"At the hotel," Preston offered casually.

"Men," Darlene rolled her eyes. "I want the details."

"I came in after a long flight, she was covering a shift at the bar, I took one look at her and said, 'I have to have that woman.'" His eyes landed back on mine and his palm nudged my knee, forcing me to uncross my legs. Thank God the tablecloth was long and we sat close enough so that no one would suspect him nearly feeling me up.

I swallowed hard.

"Isn't that nice," Darlene said.

"So, how did you and Charlie meet?" I asked, trying to divert the attention from us.

The whole room went quiet and Preston's grip on my knee tightened. Even John's face registered a mix of discomfort and distaste.

"We all went to college together," Darlene answered, and took a long swallow of her wine. She started talking to Charlie and John, making it clear she had no more desire to speak with me.

I looked at Preston. He leaned in and murmured in my ear. "Darlene and I used to date before she married my brother."

"Engaged." Darlene's shriek startled me. "We were engaged actually," she finished, her icy stare beaming at Preston over her wine glass. Charlie was staring his own daggers at Darlene and I felt like I was just kicked in the kidneys.

That explained the feeling I got from her earlier, but now I was reeling over how to deal with it. Thankfully, the waiter came with the first course and broke the staring contest. John started talking with Preston about business dealings while Charlie chimed in here and there.

Apparently, business talk was now a favorable discussion and several courses of wine and dinner went by quickly. And I was fine with that. Charlie kept eyeing me like I was a carrier of the plague. Maybe this would be a good time to try to be nice and tap into his non-asshole side.

"I hear you just had a baby, congratulations." I said to Charlie.

"Thank you. She's wonderful."

I would have thought a doting parent to be more elated but never having a baby myself, I didn't know. Both of them seemed meh about the fact that they had daughter.

"What's her name?" I asked, hoping this would help.

"Beatrice."

"That's such a pretty name."

"Yes. Well, speaking of children, we may as well tell them." Darlene grabbed Charlie's arm. "We're trying for another baby."

"So soon?" John asked. "Beatrice is only three months old."

"We want a big family." Darlene smiled at John, then at me.

"Well, congratulations again." I took a sip of wine, seriously feeling like the couple across the table from me made a stop into crazy town before arriving tonight. Everything with them was awkward and I felt as though I was constantly missing some important details. It was tough to keep up with the backward looks and insinuations.

"When are you two going to start trying for a little one?" John asked.

I started stuttering but Preston was calm as ever, like he was expecting this entire conversation.

"We'd like to be married for at least a year before we start thinking about a family. Right, sweetheart?"

I nodded.

"That makes sense." John nodded and ate his food.

"Yes, but just know we have the boy's named pick out so no taking John Charles," Darlene said with a slight laugh, but she obviously was serious.

Ah, now it made sense. They wanted a boy. The whole lineage family name crap. Were they that sexist? I had only just met John but he didn't come across like a misogynistic prick.

"I can respect a man wanting to wait and enjoy his wife," John said and raised his wine glass at Preston.

I didn't miss the glare on Charlie's face and I don't think Preston did either.

"And when you're done with your wife, you move on to someone else, isn't that right, father?" Charlie said and downed his glass of wine. I wasn't counting, but he had to be on his fifth glass and his words were definitely slurring a bit.

"That's enough, Charlie," John snapped.

"Megan and I both have a long day tomorrow meeting with the planner so we're going to get going." Preston urged me up.

"Wait, we didn't even get to see her ring yet," Darlene said quickly.

"Oh, ah..." I rubbed my bare ring finger. "I must have forgot to put it on."

All eyes zeroed in on me, but the most heated, savage pair belonged to Preston.

"You *forgot* your engagement ring?" Darlene was all smiles, clearly loving this.

"Goodnight," Preston bit out and guided me to the exit. His hand was like a brand on my lower back and anger radiated from him like a pressure cooker. I felt like a child and I knew as soon as we got to the car I was in serious trouble.

11

"What kind of woman *forgets* a half-a-million dollar diamond ring?" Preston snapped as the town car pulled into traffic. There was tinted glass between us and the driver, compliments of Preston's tastes.

"I'm sorry, but you could have prepared me for that." I hiked my thumb at the restaurant we pulled away from. "You said this agreement was built on trust. When were you going to tell me about Darlene Mc-huge-boobs in there?"

Preston grabbed my left knee and swung me around so that my back was pressed against the car door and the bottom of my heel was on the seat. I scrambled to pull down my dress because his quick snag caused my legs to spread wide. He just scooted closer and kept a firm grip on my knee.

"Are you jealous?" He grinned and glanced between my thighs. He was purposefully keeping my legs apart, flashing my panties at him. Which were getting wetter. "I do love this dress on you."

He was distracting me, but I had way too many questions to play that game…even though he may be winning already.

"I'm not jealous, I'm just surprised." Okay, maybe a little jealous, but mostly surprised.

"Uh-huh." He ran both hands up my inner thighs. I was trapped and helpless. Every time I tried to close my legs, he just gripped me hard. I was no match against his strength.

"I want to know, Preston," I breathed, and wish I sounded more convincing.

"Alright." He leaned in and placed one palm on the widow glass by the side of my face and the other stayed between my legs. His fingers traced the edge of my panties and gently brushed past them. I gasped and wiggled closer. But he kept his touch slow and soft. When his fingertip rubbed my clit I arched and moaned.

No. I wanted to know what the hell had happened in there. But I wanted his touch so bad it was splitting me apart. I snapped my eyes open.

"Preston…tell me…"

"I hate talking about the past. It's useless. Why not stay here in the present…"

He teased the opening of my pussy and I bit my bottom lip. God, I wanted to stay in the present too, but damn it, I had to stay strong. He promised me the truth and if I was going to go along with this contract and play the dutiful fiancé, knowing the kind of man he was and why members of his family were crazy, was kind of a need-to-know thing.

"I want to know you," I whispered, and gripped the lapels of his jacket.

"Fine." He shoved his big finger inside me, instantly filling me up. I groaned and fisted his jacket tighter. "I dated Darlene in college." His breath hit my mouth. "I fell for her, but when she realized I was the younger bastard son of the Strauss name—" He withdrew and returned with two fingers. My nails dug into my palms between the fabric I was gripping. "She traded up. Went after Charlie. Charlie always had a thing for her and loved that he beat me and won her."

He thrust hard. In and out, his voice growing raspy as a fire sizzled my blood. "They were pissed when they found out that Dad wasn't set on his first-born to be his heir, rather the one with the best legacy."

He sank those fingers impossibly deep and curled them, rubbing against the sensitive spot inside. My inner walls squeezed and I moved my hips up to meet him.

"Jesus, Megan." He flicked his fingers faster.

I cupped his face, bringing him so close that I took in the air he expelled and he took mine. Still fully clothed and breathing for each other, it was the most intense feeling I'd ever known.

"They think that having a son will secure everything for them," he continued, and twisted his hand, rotating those thick fingers inside me. A wild shiver broke over my skin like shattering glass and I about came undone.

I tried to focus on Preston's words. He was feeding me the information I asked for and likely wouldn't repeat himself. Fighting the urge to come and process what he said, Charlie and Darlene's behavior made a bit more sense. They were eager to tell everyone about trying for another baby because they wanted a boy.

"I may be the bastard son," Preston growled and plunged in and out faster. "But I earned my keep and they know it."

The way he spoke, with so much conviction while mastering my body, made me want to kiss every inch of him. My heart raced and my body hummed like a plucked wire.

"Preston…" His name was a whisper on my lips. A plea. I was falling, so hard and fast I couldn't cling to a thing or steady myself. My pulse thumped loudly in my temples. I didn't know the whole story behind his upbringing and my mind couldn't work quickly enough to churn out the questions I desperately wanted to ask. This was probably his goal: say his piece while rendering me speechless.

"They didn't see the wild card up my sleeve though." He kissed my chin. "You."

Stirring his fingers deep, over and over, he brushed his thumb over my clit. A small jolt caused my body to ricochet from the intense shot of pleasure. I stared at his smoldering green eyes. It was like gazing into a vat of liquefied emeralds.

"You're so wet." He kissed me quick, a single stroke of his tongue inside my mouth. "So fucking hot and responsive."

He pressed hard on my clit and kept up his assault on my pussy. The pleasure was so good it bordered on pain. Still cupping his face in my hands, I forced my touch to remain gentle and not scratch him.

"You're more beautiful and different than any other woman I've known." He turned his head within my grasp just enough to kiss my palm. "Do you hear me, Megan?"

I nodded.

He grinned. "Good."

He withdrew his fingers completely then rammed them back. I came instantly.

An ocean of searing hot tremors whipped through my body like a volcanic boomerang. It was so much, too much, still not enough. I screamed and dug my heel into the seat, likely puncturing the leather. Hot fire shot from my core to my fingertips and soldered every place in between. He was everywhere. Surrounded me with his presence.

With my eyes squeezed shut, the whole world fell away and all I felt was Preston.

12

Preston shut the penthouse door behind us and tossed his keys, not bothering to hit anything other than the floor. He took off his jacket and began unbuttoning his shirt.

"Take off your dress," he said looking at me. I backed away from him. My body was still humming from the car ride and my mind was a wreck trying to figure this man out.

One moment he was gentle, looking at me like I was the most precious thing in the world. There was an edge of truth in everything he said that compelled me to believe him when he spoke. Then there was the clinical, hard exterior, tight-lipped version that didn't give anything away and made me feel like I really was just a pawn in his chess game.

Then there was *this* Preston...

"You want me," I whispered.

It was a mindless notion, but I saw it on his face. The fire in his eyes. *That* look.

I knew he wanted me—hoped he did. I was learning his demeanor quickly and reading him was getting easier. But I wanted to hear him say it. Needed to. Because what I was feeling for him was traveling beyond the other side of "want," and it was starting to scare me.

There was an unspoken connection between us. Some things needed explaining, others were left for later. We seemed to understand that reasonably well. One thing I was picking up on was that while Preston was honest, he had secrets. I just had to know how to ask the right questions to get them out. This was a business deal after all. An elegant game. One didn't offer up something for free, that much I have learned.

"Do you enjoy hearing me state the obvious, sweetheart?" His tone held a slight playfulness but his expression was dead serious. He peeled open his shirt, leaving smooth skin and muscles and oh my…a tent in his pants that made my mouth water.

Focus!

"I want something from you," I said, running my fingers between my breasts.

"Of course you do."

"I want time. You and I. Tomorrow. Just us."

He paused and looked at me. If I wanted more of Preston, I needed to get to know him. Show him I was trustworthy beyond our agreement because there was a lot hidden beneath his exterior that I wanted to uncover. And if tonight was any indicator, there was a lot I wasn't informed about.

"Done."

I smiled and reached behind me to unzip my dress. I let the front skate across my arms and down, skimming a little past my hips, then let the material fall to the floor.

It sounded like he muttered, "Jesus Christ."

I was feeling particularly sexy because the light yellow silk bra and panties matched the dress I had worn. I unpinned my hair and let it fall loose down my back. It hit me then—the reason I was feeling confident had nothing to do with my lingerie. It was his gaze on me. *He* made me feel sexy. Beautiful. Wanted.

"Your legs…" He walked my direction then hit his knees right before me. "So fucking long." He ran his palm from my shin to my thigh. "Look at all this creamy skin." He leaned in and placed a hot kiss on my knee, then trailed his tongue higher. "Like vanilla cream."

Looking up my body he bit my inner thigh and I jumped a little. He was doing it again. Making my brain completely at odds with my body. He knelt before me like he was worshiping me. Cherishing me. I almost sobbed because it was such a good feeling.

His warmth, his praise, his attention. He was here with me, completely and totally. Silently reminding me that I wasn't alone. I felt the same way after the night in his office when we signed the contract. Even more so after the Amory event. That was why the next morning threw me. Hurt me. Because it was so different. That distance had crept back between us.

I shook my head, forcing the thoughts away. I had his time tomorrow. He couldn't run. And if he tried to keep a distance, I'd still have him in the same room and at least get some questions answered. For now, this was enough, because hopefully this was progress.

I ran my fingers through his hair and whispered, "Take me to bed."

Looking up at me and grinning, he clamped his arms around my knees and shot to his feet, throwing me over his shoulder like a sack of potatoes. I shrieked in surprise. He walked to the bed and tossed me down.

I sat up, supporting my weight with my hands on the mattress behind me and stretched my legs out.

"Take off your pants," I said.

He stood at the end of the bed and raised an eyebrow. "Ordering me around now?"

"Just a suggestion. It would be helpful for you to be naked for what I have in mind," I teased, deliberately flicking my tongue to taste my lips.

A deep rumble broke from his chest as he unfastened his belt and removed his pants. Standing in all his glory was every edible inch of Preston Strauss, but there were several inches I wanted to taste first.

"Come here." I reclined backward, resting my weight on my forearms.

He climbed onto the bed. The dark gleam in his eyes was that of a man intrigued. Preston didn't get ordered around a lot, but in this moment, he let me issue the commands.

Crawling up my body, his knees on either side of my legs, he didn't stop until he was at my hips.

"I said, come *here*." I lifted my chin. He scooted higher up my body until he straddled my chest and his impressive cock bobbed right in front of my face. Giving him the wickedest smile I could, I locked my eyes on his and opened my mouth.

"You asked me once if this was real…" He fisted his cock and ran the crown along my lower lip. "Now I'm the one wondering if this is a dream."

I flicked my tongue out and tasted him. Hot steel encased in velvet. He removed his hand, resting his cock on my open mouth, so I closed it around him and sucked hard. He hissed and threaded his fingers through my hair.

"Fuck, you're amazing."

Pressing further, I took more of him, raining my tongue along the underside of his cock as I went. The grip he had in my hair was tightening. Not enough to hurt me, but I knew he was on the brink. I wanted to be that for him. The place he could lose himself in.

I retreated, leaving a shiny trail on his thick length, proof of where I had been. Laving at the tip, I sucked the crown just enough to get his hips rocking toward me, seeking more. Exactly what I was going for.

"Take me," I said, and gave a loving kiss on his beautiful cock. He frowned down at me, gently massaged my scalp, as if silently gauging my seriousness.

"Take me," I said again, licking him from base to tip, then opened my mouth once more. Waiting for him. "However you want."

With a firm grasp on either side of my head, he slowly pushed his hips forward, impaling his cock between my lips. Breathing through my nose, I relaxed every muscle. He must have felt it because he pressed deeper. The crown bumped against the back of my throat and he groaned.

"Look at you." He stroked his thumb along my cheekbone. "Taking me deep."

He pulled almost all the way out then thrust back inside. I moaned around him. My pussy clenched for something to fill me, but there was only emptiness.

"You like this?" He moved in and out, slowly at first, then picking up pace. "Me fucking this pretty mouth of yours?"

I nodded and sucked at him greedily. A thin sheen of sweat broke over his tan chest and every inward glide caused his abdominals to flex so hard they nearly cut out of his skin. My God, he was gorgeous. The way he moved was like watching live art and I had a front row seat.

I tilted my head back even further, allowing for deeper access.

"Fuck, sweetheart, you're going to make me come." His eyes locked on mine and I nodded again. Telling him it was okay to stay right where he was.

His hard dick twitched and Preston's entire body wracked tight with so much tension, there wasn't a relaxed slice of muscle anywhere on him. Holding himself to the hilt, his hot release coated my throat and I swallowed around him, drinking him down.

"Goddess," he whispered.

When the last of his shudders eased, he slowly withdrew and I lapped up every last inch of him as he pulled from my mouth.

He scooted down my body and kicked my thighs open with his knees.

"What are you doing?" I said, trying to catch my breath.

He positioned himself at my core and surged inside. I gasped.

"H-how are you still—" My words cut off because he thrust again, so determined it made my teeth clatter and the orgasm that had been simmering beneath the surface rise quickly.

"You, sweetheart," he growled. "You keep me hard."

He was unyielding. Driving into me over and over, hitting every nerve ending until I lost all awareness of everything except Preston. There was no build-up. No easy accumulation of pleasure. I lost myself so completely to the sudden onset of his pistoning hips that white light blinked behind my eyes.

"Oh, God, yes!" My climax exploded, intense and fast, rocking my entire being from the ends of my limbs to the center of my soul. Preston had branded me with his heat and overpowered me with his will.

Trying to breathe. Trying so hard to locate reality, I laid there, clutching to him, not wanting this moment to end.

13

I stretched and buried my head deeper into the pillow, which was hard and smelled like a yummy man and sex.

"You're killing me, sweetheart."

The rumbling accompanied with that deep voice affirmed that it wasn't a pillow at all, it was Preston's impressive chest.

"Well, you killed me last night," I mumbled and nipped his torso. His arm tightened around me.

"I hope not." He trailed his hand down to my ass and squeezed. "Since I opted to stay in bed and forgo my routine, I'm in need of exercise this morning."

He flipped me to my back and was on top me in one quick movement. I giggled like a fool but clutched him closer. Cradled between my thighs, he sunk inside of me. Sighing deeply, I let happiness and contentment wash over me.

This was a great way to start the morning.

We walked beneath florescent lights, dodging strollers and shoppers while licking our ice cream cones.

"Of all things to do, you brought me to an outlet mall?" Preston said.

"I know it's hard for someone like you to understand money-bags, but wandering around with no agenda, people watching and eating ice cream is fun."

He smiled down at me and wove his fingers with mine. Since we woke up this morning, everything had been pleasantly peaceful. Like we were a real couple. He wasn't distant or even harsh. I didn't want spoil today with questions I knew he didn't want to answer but they were gnawing away at me.

"So," I started as we passed Banana Republic. "Your dad seems really great."

Preston nodded. "He is."

Not quite the response I was hoping for.

"How was it growing up with him?"

He frowned at me. "What kind of question was that?"

I shrugged. "I don't know. Just wondering how your child-hood was? You and your brother don't seem to get along. Was that always the case?"

"My brother and I never got along. We hadn't even met until I was thirteen and I went to live with my father."

"You never visited you dad before then?"

"Of course I did. He was around a fair amount actually. I just never met his other family."

I knew that based on what he said and the way his Charlie had behaved at dinner the other night, Preston was the child out of wedlock due to an affair. But I didn't know the whole story. We continued walking and I licked at my cone a bit.

"Did your mom know he was married?"

"Yes."

"So they got along, your mom and dad?"

"She was in love with him."

His tone was getting terser and his answers quick and sharp. Getting him to talk was like pulling teeth. I was treading danger-ously close to a total Preston shutdown.

"Can I ask you one more thing?"

"You can ask me anything you want, doesn't mean you'll like my response."

Yep, I was losing him. Time to back off.

"Never mind."

He stopped and gripped my hand. "I don't like games, Megan."

"It's not a game, I just...I don't want to ruin today."

Something in his face softened and he brought my hand to his mouth and kissed it.

"I don't either. Talking about my past isn't pleasant. But I understand your curiosity. You didn't read all about it like I did with yours."

"Yeah." The thought that Preston knew all about Tim, my parents, my past...It was embarrassing as much as liberating. I couldn't hide from him, and yet, he still chose me.

"My father had an affair with my mother and I was the result. They kept up this charade of a secret relationship for several years until she died. I went to live with him. He's always treated me well, even though his wife never liked me for obvious reasons and when she passed away a few years ago, things got really bad with Charlie. I worked for my stake in the company while his was handed to him. But once Charlie's mother died, my father started talking about changing the will and Charlie's been gunning ever since."

I nodded, appreciating his honesty. He spoke quickly and bluntly as if wanting to move past the topic. I couldn't really blame him.

"Thank you for telling me."

My phone buzzed. I pulled it out and didn't recognize the number.

"Hello?"

"Megan, it's Darlene, I was hoping we could have lunch on Wednesday."

"Oh." I looked at Preston who was frowning at me. I mouthed *Darlene* and pointed at the phone. He clenched his jaw. "Ah, sure. Lunch is fine."

"Great. I'll just pop by the hotel at noon."

"Okay, bye." I hung up.

"Looks like I'm having lunch with Darlene on Wednesday."

"Lucky you." Preston took my hand to continue our leisurely walk. There was so much more I wanted to know. But I was pretty sure I had already met my quota of information Preston would dish out in one day.

"How did she even get my number?" I asked.

"Who knows? But I wouldn't put much past her."

"Creepy."

"Yep." He stopped and pulled me closer. "I think we should go in there."

I looked across the way and saw Victoria's Secret. I didn't even answer before he was damn near tugging me toward the bright pink storefront.

"Oh yeah," he said, looking around like a kid in a candy shop. "This *is* going to be fun."

●　●　●

I shimmied into another garment that Preston had picked out for me. He was surprisingly patient for a man shopping, but I was showing him all the "outfits" so he couldn't complain much.

He sat right outside my dressing room and somehow talked the sales lady into giving us complete privacy. After giggling and fiddling with her hair, she closed off one whole batch of rooms so we could be alone. It was nice to know that Preston's charm didn't just work on me.

I heard him speaking, but couldn't make out the words. I adjusted the French maid-inspired pink and black get-up and slipped my black heels back on for effect. When I opened the door he looked at me and—

Was that my cell phone he was talking into?

"Hang on just a second, Kate, she's right here. It was nice talking to you too."

My whole face went cold and I knew blood must have drained from it. Preston confidently rose from his perch and handed me my phone.

"By the way," he looked me over and traced his fingers over my thigh, "this one is a keeper."

I swallowed hard and put the phone to my ear.

"Kate?"

"Oh my God, Megan! You're getting married and you didn't tell me? I called you to see what was going on and your fiancé answers the phone and…just…wow!"

"I ah…it just sort of happened." I glared at Preston who went back to sit down and looked at me with the smuggest grin I've ever seen a man wear.

"Well, I understand how that goes, but…is everything okay. I mean, are you okay?"

"Yes, I'm good."

There was a pause and I knew poor Kate was struggling. She cared. I knew she did and I would have been floored, hell, I was floored, when she told me she and Adam were engaged all those months ago.

"Are you happy, Meg? Does he make you happy?" Her tone was soft, doing the same thing I would have—gauging my reaction.

"He does." I left out, "most of the time."

"Well, okay then. This is amazing! I had no idea you were even dating someone. But Preston filled me in a little. He sounds great."

"He's something alright," I grated between clenched teeth.

"He said you were waiting to tell everyone and nervous because it's all happened so fast but Meg, I'm so happy for you. I'd never judge you, you know that right?"

My heart hurt a little. I did know that. But this situation was complicated and I had waited to tell Kate not because I didn't think she'd be supportive, but because I didn't want to lie to her. And omitting the details that this was a contractual thing was technically lying.

"You aren't going to tell me that this is happening too fast?"

"With anyone else, I might," Kate sighed. "But this is you, Meg. If you say he's the one and you're happy, then I'm not going to tell you otherwise. Sometimes love just sneaks up on you." I could hear the smile in her voice and once again was so happy she and Adam had found each other. But the word "love" and Kate's unconditional support tore at my chest like a fresh wound, and the guilt was already starting to fester.

"Thanks, Kate. I ah, I want to talk more about this but I'm kind of," I looked down my body, "indisposed at the moment, can I call you tonight?"

"Of course! You have to call me."

"Promise I will."

"Okay, bye!"

"Bye."

I hung up the phone and threw it at Preston. He caught it effortlessly and smiled. "Ooh, looks like I'll have to punish the maid for throwing a tantrum," he teased.

"I can't believe you told her."

"I can't believe you haven't told anyone. A man might think you're ashamed of him."

I looked at the ceiling and begged for patience. "I told Emma."

"Because you had to."

"I was waiting on everyone else. Planning my moment."

"Uh-huh, well with the wedding coming up quick, I suggest you get on that."

"I will."

"Good."

He twirled his finger. "Now, let me see the back."

"You're joking, right?"

"Nope, let me see the goods, sweetheart." He winked and I couldn't help but hide my smile. He was so cute when he was at ease and playful like this. But I still feigned being somewhat upset. Part of me was grateful Kate knew.

I spun in a slow circle and Preston took a rough breath. When I turned back around his eyes were still on me but he was pulling out his own cell phone from his pocket.

"What are you doing?"

"Calling the hotel. I think I just found the new housekeeping uniforms."

● ● ●

I took a deep breath and walked into the hotel restaurant. Darlene was sitting at a small table in the corner. Four days to prepare and I still wasn't ready to face her.

"Hi there." She stood and kissed my cheek.

Weird. My friend Kate was the one with space issues, but right then I understood not liking someone too close to your face. Especially when you were pretty sure that person was harboring some serious claws.

"How are you, Darlene?"

We both sat. I opted to go for a causal look in jeans and a pink sweater. Darlene however was dressed to the nines in another tight red number with a plunging neckline. I was seeing quickly how attention tended to divert down when speaking to her.

"I'm great! I just thought we should get to know each other, you know, sister to sister."

Something about the way she said that made a gross taste rise in my mouth and it wasn't this relentless flu bug I had been fighting recently. Feeling exhausted almost all the time now was bringing on dizzy spells and I had little patience for games. I wasn't an idiot and it was obvious Darlene wasn't happy about me marrying Preston.

Preston however had no desire for Darlene. I replayed last night in my mind when we tested out the new maid uniform. I believed Preston when he told me things. Darlene wasn't a threat…not in a sexual way at least. Everyone had a past and this woman was not atop my "people I like" list but she was going to be my—gulp—sister-in-law. No sense in adding to the awkwardness. The fact that she was a ragging bizzo was apparent and accounted for.

"That's nice of you." I smiled.

The waiter came and took our order. Salad and mimosa for Darlene and chicken for me.

"So, you and Preston seem to have happened pretty fast."

Here we go. This wasn't a get-to-know-you session, this was an interrogation. One thing I was learning from Preston was that the truth could be taken a lot of different ways, but it was still the truth. Keep it vague without it being a lie. Guess it was my turn to test his tactics.

"Really fast," I said. "Like, 'what's your name, wanna get married?' kind of fast." I smiled wide, loving how the truth—sort of—felt good to say.

Darlene didn't seem as amused.

"So you must be really thrilled that John is giving Preston his three percent as a wedding present?" she hissed. My mouth hung open and shock tingled along my spine. "Oh, did I spoil the surprise?"

"I didn't know John had made a decision."

"I find it interesting that Preston turned up to be engaged so suddenly and even more odd is that the wedding is happening so soon."

"We have our reasons for that," I muttered, trying for confidence but not wanting to go into those "reasons," like my father's illness, with this woman. Or the other fact that Preston did want to get married because of the three percent. It looked like Darlene wasn't an idiot herself. She was obviously a schemer. The way she played Preston was enough for me to dislike her.

"Oh, I'm sure you do. Preston, he always has a plan after all. Don't think that I'm blind to that or that I am going to let John sign over the stake of the company to him. Charlie is the oldest, *legitimate* son. And married or not, I know the kind of man Preston is. He's never going to produce a family. Whatever you're up to, I'll find out."

Okay, that's it. "What goes on between Preston and I is none of your business. And what John decides to do is up to him. I don't care what you *think* you know about Preston, because he's not yours to think about."

"Oh, look at you. Defending him like you mean it."

I understood right then Emma's obsession with bitch-slapping. Because in that moment, there was nothing I wanted more than to smack Darlene. Fine, she had a hunch that something was up and that was technically true. But she had played her hand with Preston a long time ago and lost. Despite how our relationship started, I cared about Preston, and whatever Darlene was aiming to do wasn't good.

"He must not have caught you up on all the family gossip if you're still this hung up on him." She ran her fingertip along the rim of her glass and the evil glare in her eye made me feel really, really uncomfortable—like at any moment she was going to poison me with her mere words.

"I think I'm pretty well caught up," I went to stand but her words stilled me.

"So he told you about his mom?"

I nodded. "Yeah. I know that his father stepped out of the marriage and Preston and Charlie have different moms."

She pursed her lips and eyed me. "No, I don't mean about the fact that John cheated. I'm talking about what *happened* to Preston's mom."

"She passed away."

The grin on Darlene's face could only be classified as pure evil. She leaned in and licked her lips like she was ready to devour a helpless baby deer.

"I'm not surprised he didn't give you details. Preston doesn't open up to many people. But…"

Rage started to boil and I reminded myself that this was a sad, scorned woman who passed on a great guy like Preston for Junior Mc-Stink-Eye and was obviously upset about it now. Especially now the coveted three percent was being dangled in front of her.

"I think you should know what went on since you'll have to live with Preston's…fits." She took a drink of her mimosa.

I sat back down. "Fits?"

She nodded. "Every year on the anniversary of his mother's death, Preston goes into rages. Drinks excessively. Acts crazy. It was amazing I got out of there untouched."

Wait, what? Was she insinuating what I think she was?

"Are you claiming something about Preston? Because if you are, I'd think long and hard before you say things that aren't true." A super pissed-off pitch coated my words. I was done with her and this maliciousness. That she would even hint that Preston would ever hurt her, or any other woman, was absurd.

"Calm down, I didn't say anything. No, Preston never hit me. I'm just saying he gets crazy."

Oh, I think I was currently staring down the barrel of crazy. I had grown up with Kate and been around her bipolar mother a few times to unfortunately see what rage looks like in a person. The look in someone's eyes before they struck was something you could never forget. Preston wasn't that person. He was private, but not hateful.

"I'm sure Preston would tell me if there was an issue."

Darlene scoffed. "He didn't even tell you how she died."

I frowned. Darlene clearly had more information than I did and couldn't wait to spill. So she didn't.

"The woman killed herself. Slit her wrists in the bathtub. Preston was thirteen when he walked in and found her." Darlene leaned back and waved her hand in the air. "He pulled her out, tried to save her but she had been dead for hours. Blood everywhere. Total scandal."

My mouth hung open and Darlene looked almost excited and happy to be talking about this. "Why in the hell would you say something like that?" My voice was somewhere between a growl and a whisper.

"Because it's true." She shrugged and forked her salad.

"No." I snapped my finger at her and she had the grace to look me in the eye. "I mean, why would you say it that way, like it's a piece of gossip?"

"I'm doing you a favor, Megan. I just thought you should know what you're getting into. Whatever Preston promised you, it isn't worth his dark moments."

"Oh, I'm very clear on what I'm getting into." I set my napkin on the table and stood. "If you have a soul at all, you'd be wise to not talk about Preston, or his mother's memory, like that again."

She stared at me and I didn't bother letting her speak. I just walked away. Rushing to the elevator, I prayed Preston would be at the penthouse or the office. I needed to talk to him. Now.

14

Things were making more and more sense. Preston's reaction to the bathtub and his method of vague truth. I searched the penthouse. He wasn't there so I walked across the hall to the office and rushed in. There were two men in suits sitting on the other side of his desk and all three sets of eyes landed on me.

"Megan." Preston stood and so did both the men. "Everything okay?"

I swallowed hard. He looked legitimately concerned and to be honest, no, everything was not okay. I wasn't one for the dramatics but I didn't think I could wait to talk to him.

"Gentlemen," he looked at my face then at the men, "can you give me and my fiancé a few moments please."

The men mumbled, "Of course" and showed themselves out.

Preston apologized and shut the door behind them. He was on me in two long-legged strides cupping my shoulders.

"What's wrong?"

I shook my head. "Darlene…"

Preston's hands dropped and he looked at the ceiling. "Christ, what did she do?"

I frowned at the ground. I had no idea how to proceed. How to tell him what she had said. He should know, right? That she was saying these things? And because it was so awful I wanted to comfort him or tell him it was okay. I wanted to do something. Anything! My mind just wouldn't spit anything out.

"Megan. We went over this last night and again this morning. I told you she would try to mess with your mind and use our past to hurt you. But she's nothing. I don't—"

"I know. She didn't tell me about you two. She told me that your father was going to sign over the three percent to you as a wedding present. Then she questioned our relationship. Said she was going to find out what was really going on. Did you know about this?"

"I spoke with my father this morning. It's good news but was bound to upset Charlie and Darlene. She's grasping for anything to help her case."

"Preston, I…she hit me with so much."

He glanced at his watch, completely unaffected. "Everything is fine, Megan."

"Everything is not fine, Preston. She told me about your mother."

He took a step back and I looked up at him. His face was hard as marble. "You barged in here, interrupted a meeting with foreign executives, because of that?"

"Preston, it's a big deal. Darlene was so…harsh about it. She said you found your mother and—"

"Enough!" I snapped my mouth shut. "If this was something I wanted to discuss, don't you think I would have?"

"I don't know. That's the problem. I have no idea what you would or wouldn't tell me."

He flexed his jaw. "Really? I did a background check on you and I know what I need to know. But I never pressed you for details. You want to tell me about Tim?" His sinister tone could have cut me half. "Do you want to tell me how much of your parents' current situation is really your fault? You want to tell me just how close you got to your ex-boss and exactly *what* you did for him?"

Breath left my lungs at the low blow. Anger and sadness washed over me. If he was trying to hurt me on purpose, he just did a hell of a job.

"I didn't do nearly as much for him as I'm doing for my current boss," I snarled the last word.

In that one sentence, I had let Preston paint me my worst nightmare. I felt cheap and stupid. Tim had kissed me and I tried to stop it. Regret didn't begin to explain how terrible I felt about it. And even worse, I talked my parents into dealing with him. It was the same reason Preston used to his advantage over me right now. I was in a lose-lose situation. He and I both knew it.

"I came here because I was worried about you," I said, forcing back tears, which popped up out of nowhere. "You didn't prep me on how to handle information about your past."

"I didn't think Darlene knew the fucking details," he growled and stood behind his desk.

I tried to dodge all the negativity flying around the room and focus on what my goal was. I came here out of instinct. Preston was my concern.

"I just wanted to make sure—"

"Make sure what, Megan?"

"She said a lot of things, Preston. And I just wanted to see you, is all."

"Oh yeah?" He walked around his desk, slowly drawing in on me with each step. Intentionally prolonging the torture like a lion circling its prey. "I don't give a shit what she says about the past or the present. I don't want to hear it, nor is it your place to come in here and think you have any right to my business, personal or otherwise."

I shook my head. "She said things about *you* Preston. Said that you have fits of rage."

He stepped closer.

"And you believe her." It wasn't a question. It was a statement. One I rejected quickly.

I shot my chin in the air and looked him dead in the eye. He was not my favorite person at the moment, but even now, one thing remained true.

"I'm not afraid of you, Preston."

Step.

"No?"

I shook my head. "I didn't and don't believe her. I was shocked and wanted to come see you. That's it. I'm not forcing you to talk or even acknowledge anything, but I'm here if you want to."

I turned to leave. He grabbed my arm and I stopped, turning to look at him over my shoulder. Fiery anger shot through his eyes, but behind that mask was a hint of vulnerability. There was so much hidden deep within Preston Strauss and I had a feeling I had only scratched the surface of a long-standing nightmare. This was more than I was prepared for and in that moment, I had no idea what to do or why I had signed up for this mess in the first place.

"Why are you doing this, Megan?"

"I was just asking myself the same thing."

15

"Megan, honey, are you okay? You sound upset." My mother's voice on the line was the kindest thing I'd heard in a long time.

I sat on my bed in my apartment. It was cold and still, but I was happy I had somewhere to go. Emma wasn't home and from the looks of it, hadn't been for a night or two.

"I'm fine mom, just tired. How are you? How's Daddy?"

She sighed. "I'm fine. Daddy is…well he's doing alright."

I pinched the bridge of my nose. I knew that tone. It had been several days since I had talked with her last. Since our conversation with the doctor several weeks ago, our conversations had been brief—one of which was telling her more cash would be wired weekly. I had gotten off the phone before she could argue.

"Are you getting the money?"

"About that Megan, I don't want you putting yourself out. I am looking for some part-time work and I'm sure everything will be fine. You need to take care of you."

"No, Mom. You're retired. And there's enough coming that it will take care of the house payments and hire someone full time to come take care of Daddy. Please Mom, just accept it. Take care of you and Daddy with it. It's not hurting me at all to send it."

I heard my poor mother sob and I couldn't help but choke back tears myself. I knew right then why I had agreed to this whole contract in the first place. The reasons were on the other end of the phone. It was just a messy accident that the contract came with a difficult man who I was falling for.

"Now, enough about the money," I said wiping my eyes. "I want to hear more about you and Daddy. Are the exercises the doctor recommended helping? Are you getting out into the garden at all?"

My mother muffled what sounded like a tissue and let me have my way in changing the subject.

"The petunias are blooming nicely. And we do the exercises. Some days they seem to help, but others…not so much. He's trying though. It's hard, honey. One moment he's making sense, the next he's confused or talking about past events like it's present time. The doctor said that it's just how this progresses."

"Any luck finding a nurse?"

"We've interviewed a few. Still nothing permanent yet."

I nodded even though I knew she couldn't see me. Dementia was degenerative. Sooner or later my father would lose the bulk of his mind. Every day it got worse, our only hope was to slow the process.

"Can I talk to him?"

"Of course! He'd love to hear your voice. I'll put it on speaker, okay?"

I waited a minute then heard my dad's voice. "Hello?"

"Hi, Daddy! How are you?"

"Judy dear, I'm—" he trailed off and I heard my mother murmur.

"No, I'm Judy. Megan is on the phone."

"Megan?"

"Yes, Leo. Megan. Your daughter."

Hearing my parents' discussion tore my heart out. My mother was trying to be quiet so I couldn't hear. I palmed my mouth and squeezed my eyes shut to keep from sobbing.

"D-Daddy?" I tried again. "Daddy, it's Megan."

"Meg-Pie!" A sigh of relief burst through my chest. "I miss you, kiddo. How's school going?"

"Megan graduated college a while ago. She's in New York now," my mom clarified.

"New York?"

"It's okay, Mom," I said. "I'm doing great, Daddy. How are you?"

"Oh well, you know, doing alright. Damn knee hurts. I talked to Herb yesterday about getting this doctor bill put on workman's comp since I hurt it on the job last week."

My mother didn't try to correct him this time and I didn't either. My father hadn't worked in almost eight years and his old boss Herb died before he left the company.

"I'm sorry, Daddy. I hope you feel better."

"Enough about this old man, how are you Meg-Pie? Getting good grades?"

"Yes, sir."

"That's my girl."

I laughed and tears rolled down my cheeks.

"I've got to get his dinner going," my mom said. "But you call us and keep us posted and I really don't want—"

"Mom, please, just take it. I'm going to keep sending it. Every week. Please."

She took a deep breath. "Thank you, honey."

"I love you, Mom."

"Oh, I love you too."

We hung up and the only thing I could do was drop my cell on the bed next to me, throw my face into my palms and cry.

● ● ●

Something warm and smooth skated across my cheek. I opened my eyes and saw Preston staring down at me, the back of his finger tracing along my cheekbone. I must have fallen asleep after hanging up with my mom.

I sat up and my old bed creaked a little.

"I locked the door…" I murmured, still sleepy and dazed.

"Yeah, I had a key made," he said, and sat next to me.

"What's mine is yours," I mumbled.

Too exhausted to fight. My stomach kind of hurt and my eyes felt puffy and my body ached as though I had been sleeping in a cave. Cold and alone. Because I had been.

Heat radiated from Preston and he smelled so good. I wanted to curl up in his arms but there was still a dark cloud between us. After the last several weeks I felt like we had made progress, and now this setback felt like it put an eternity between us.

"How did you find me?"

His thumb trailed along my cheekbone. "You've been crying."

I ran the back of my hand over my eye.

"When you weren't anywhere at the hotel," he murmured, "I figured this would be the next place you'd go."

I guess I wasn't that hard to track down.

"I'm tired, Preston." He nodded. "But I'm not sorry about arrangement. I'm confused and you drive me kind of crazy, but I'm not sorry. I haven't lied to you. I can't handle being treated the way you treated me."

He sat on the bed next to me and faced me. "I know." His jaw clenched like he was going to say more. So I stayed quiet, hoping he would. Finally he looked me in the eye. "I wasn't prepared for what Darlene did. But it's no excuse for what I said to you."

"Thank you," I whispered.

He cupped my face. "I've been honest with you too."

"I know you have, you've just been vague."

He nodded and looked away. His green eyes were haunted and I wanted to reach out and hug him. There was so much behind every expression.

I loved my parents dearly. Losing one of them would crush my world. I was losing my father in a sense and it was slowly wrecking me. But to go through what Preston did, see his mother the way he had…I don't know how he coped. He probably didn't even have a chance to process the loss before he was thrown into a situation where he was the "bastard son." It must have been terrible.

"I won't force you to share details if you don't want to." I grabbed his free hand and squeezed.

"I grew up a certain way," he said, and glanced down at our woven hands. "I know better than to trust someone completely, especially with something important, something that could weaken you. It's just unwise."

I forced back the tears because I saw it on his face right then and it made sense.

A child trusted their parent to take care of them. To support them. To never leave them. It was an unspoken, understood rule. To have that broken did damage, which was why Preston liked his contracts and play-by-play deals.

It also made a remark of Darlene's stand out: "Preston will never have family." His feelings about children obviously went beyond the contract and the pregnancy void clause.

"I grew up hated in my father's home. Every move I made was like shifting a game piece. I don't like people having information on me and the upper hand. I don't like the unexpected happening."

"I understand."

He kissed my left palm and placed it on his chest. Something cold slid down my ring finger. I looked down to see Preston place the blue diamond engagement ring onto my finger.

"*You*, Megan, are unexpected." He leaned in and brushed his lips across mine. "And it scares the hell out of me."

He kissed me hard and deep and I melted for him. This day was a rollercoaster of emotions. Feeling Preston's honesty and warmth was all I needed. I hoisted myself up on my knees and threw my arms around him. I kissed him with everything I felt, everything that was hurting me. Everything that made me cry and everything that made me smile. I put it all into that kiss. Because he brought it *all* out.

"You feel good," he breathed against my mouth, and I wasn't sure he even realized he spoke.

"Missed you," I said back.

He nodded. This was the closeness. The connection I'd been craving. I had been spoiled and seen the side of Preston that was open and lighthearted. Attentive and consuming. Then today to be barely acknowledged was like being on the cold side of the moon. Now, tasting his lips and working each others' clothes free, I felt alive and whole. Comforted and safe.

I took his shirt off and he lifted my sweater over my head. All my hair fell in loose tangles and his big palms seized the sides of my face and he devoured my mouth with his. On our knees atop my bed, we kissed and laved, like we truly did miss this. Because I did.

A little maneuvering was all it took to get both our pants off. Preston laid me down, his mouth never leaving my skin while he worked my bra and panties off, then his boxers. From my navel to the swell of my breast he kissed and licked. Not teasing, simply stating his intentions.

"Every time," he growled and sucked on my nipple, "you look more beautiful."

I arched my back and wrapped my legs around him, coaxing him up. His mouth did amazing things to my breasts, but I was so lost for him that all I wanted was to feel him inside me.

"I need you, Preston."

He looked up, ensnaring my gaze, and slowly scooted up my body just enough so that his hard cock prodded my pelvis. I shifted my hips so that the crown lingered right at my opening. He braced himself on his forearms on either side of my head.

"I need you too…" He kissed me so softly it brought tears to my already aching eyes and he sank inside of me.

I gasped into his mouth and he breathed deep, taking all my air and robbing any kind of oxygen around me. All I felt was him. My environment, every moment surrounding me, and the world itself stopped. All that existed was him.

For a moment, as his steady exhale fanned between my lips, his body surrounding—invading—mine, all I was, was what he allowed me to be. He was the universe I was living in and I the surface that surrounded him.

"Megan…" He didn't move his body from mine. With my breasts pressed against his hard chest and my legs wrapped around him, all of our skin was touching. Never withdrawing, he shifted his hips and stirred his cock deeply. The fire he coaxed had no time to flicker, it just raged hot and began splintering my nerves like dry bark in winter. I was splitting apart. Falling and breaking. The only thing holding me together was him.

"I feel…I…" I couldn't say it. Because nothing seemed to make sense. I shouldn't feel the way I did. Not in that moment and not the same feeling that had been gnawing at me for the last week. But it was there. Hovering and seeping into me with every breath and thrust from Preston.

Love.

I never knew what making love was. Because I had never experienced it. The reason I knew that was because what was happening right then was a first. I put the word to the thoughts, but couldn't say it aloud. Not yet.

"Take me," I pleaded.

With the blue diamond catching a fleck of light and winking at me as I held Preston's face, he kissed me hard, and took me at my request.

● ● ●

It was ten in the morning and I woke up in a king-sized bed surrounded by fluffy pillows and cream sheets.

"Home," I smiled into the pillow then sat up quickly realizing what I had just mumbled out loud.

The word came out of nowhere and just like last night, startled me with the truth of it. I was in the penthouse. I vaguely remembered the car ride from my apartment in the wee hours of the morning after Preston and I had "made up."

"I'm glad you think so," Preston said, walking into the bedroom. He was freshly shaven and in light gray suit that made his caramel skin shine and his green eyes pop. He sat down on the edge of the bed and ran his fingers along my shoulder. "I have some meetings, but tonight, I've arranged for dinner. One I'm certain you'll like more than the last few I've dragged you to."

"Oh yeah?" I reached and straightened the black pocket square in his jacket.

"Yeah." He tucked a lock of hair behind my ear. "Kate, Adam and Emma are meeting us."

I shot up to my knees. "Really?"

He smiled and nodded. "I've spoken with Adam and he and Kate are flying in for a few days to spend time with you, then they'll be back in a couple weeks for the wedding."

I flung my arms around him and about knocked him off the bed. His chest rumbled with a low laugh and he hugged me tight and laid me back on the bed, following down.

"Have I told you how good you look in my shirt?" In bed with only Preston's white tee on and him fully dressed between my thighs was an erotic image. If he commanded me to stay here and wait his return in the sternest caveman voice, I just might do it.

"Thank you. So, so much." I kissed him and he returned my intentions. "I wish you could stay," I murmured between bites of his bottom lip.

"Done," he said, and took off his jacket while keeping most of his weight over me.

"What?"

"You want me to stay?" He threw the coat on the floor. "I stay."

A giddy laugh bounced out. "No, no. You're an important man with meetings."

"Megan." His big palms clasped my neck and my gaze locked to his. "You are important."

My heart lurched and the weighty blue diamond on my finger felt warmer. Realer.

"Well, I'd feel guilty if you missed work. How do you feel about a quicky?"

He grinned and kissed my lips.

"Your wish is my command."

● ● ●

After a not-so-quick quickie, Preston reluctantly left to attend business, leaving me fully sated and grinning like a moron in bed. The man never did anything halfway, that was for sure.

I smiled, grabbed my cell off the nightstand and dialed my mother.

"Hi, Mom."

"Hi, honey. You sound much better than you did last night."

"Yeah. Today is a good day. I wanted to tell you something. Is Daddy...okay to talk?"

"He ah, it's a rough day for him today."

"Oh." My shoulders slumped. I knew this was a possibility. Knew that every time I called it was a gamble and the odds weren't in my favor.

"But I'd love to hear what you have to say." My mother was chipper. "I can tell him when he's having a good day, or have him call you back?"

"Thanks, Mom. But I want to tell you."

"Everything okay?"

I smiled and nodded. "Yeah, actually everything is better than okay. I'm getting married."

"What!" Her happy shriek vibrated the entire phone. "Oh, honey, this is wonderful! I'm so sorry with everything going on with your dad I haven't asked much about you. I should have known someone had snatched up my smart pretty girl."

Heat stained my cheeks and my eyes felt heavy with happy tears.

"Tell me all about this young man I'm going to call son."

"His name is Preston and I," I sighed, "Mom, I am so in love with him it kind of hurts."

"Oh, honey." A tissue rustled over the line and between the sound and my mother's sniffles, I knew she was crying. "That's the best kind."

Running fingers through my hair I took in every elated pitch of my mother's tone and it blanketed me with comfort. And it felt good telling her. Because it was the truth.

"The wedding is actually happening pretty soon, so I was hoping to chat with you about the details of getting you and Daddy here."

"Whatever it takes, Megan. Whenever it is, we'll be there."

I couldn't hold back the warmth and happiness flooding me. For the first time, the world around me looked a bit brighter and if I wasn't careful, I just may start believing that this fairytale I was in was real.

16

"Smells amazing, sweetheart," Preston said, and came to stand behind me. He looked over my shoulder at the stovetop I was working over. "Lasagna?"

"My famous lasagna," I said with a smile.

"Can't wait." He kissed my neck and backed away. "Everyone should be showing up in about an hour."

I turned to face him. "Thank you for this Preston. All of this."

Stuffing his hand in his pockets, he glanced at the floor. "Just seemed like this was the kind of thing you needed."

"It is."

He nodded. "I'm going to change then I'll come help."

"Okay." A smile crept over my face and it had to be the millionth one today. Starting with Preston in bed, a great chat with my mother, and the truth of my feelings being out, I was so excited to end with my best friends coming over and hanging out at the place I had come to call home.

Preston offered to order food so I wouldn't have to cook but I was happy to take on the task. And he was right. I needed this. It felt right. My friends, my family, my life…all on the same page as Preston.

I was an hour and a few layers of noodles, cheese and sauce away from operation Total Integration.

"God, I've missed you!" Kate said and wrapped me in a hug, which was a bit surprising because she wasn't a hugger. In fact, Adam was the only one I've ever seen touch her regularly. But I was so happy for the embrace and clutched her close.

"I've missed you too."

She released me and damn it, I wanted to cry again. For some reason I had been doing that a lot the past few weeks. My emotions were unbalanced and I decided to blame the craziness of the wedding and, well, life.

"Hi, Megan," Adam said with a smile and kissed my cheek. "We brought wine." He handed it to me.

"Thanks. Adam, Kate, this is my fiancé Preston Strauss." Preston stepped from behind me and shook both their hands.

"We've talked on the phone but it's so nice to finally meet you in person." Kate smiled. Adam and Preston instantly started talking and Kate elbowed my side gently. "I see the appeal." She winked and I laughed.

"Let's get this open." We headed for the kitchen while the boys went into the living room. "I thought Emma was coming with you?"

"So did I," Kate said taking a deep appreciative inhale of the lasagna cooling on the counter. "But she said she didn't want us to pick her up and would meet us here. Guess she had something to do."

"Yeah, I think she's been out of town the last few days, or staying somewhere else."

"Is everything okay?"

"Far as I know. She travels for work so I assume that's it."

"Emma's never been overly open about things so you're probably right."

I got out four glasses and poured the wine. "This will be Emma's." I scooted the glass back a bit.

"You're not having any?"

I shook my head. "My stomach has been kind of finicky lately."

"You sick?"

"Must be, I've been battling a bug for the last few weeks. It's all the stress, I'm sure. But!" I handed Kate her glass. "Enough about that. Tell me all about what you and Adam have been up to."

"Oh, you know, just trying to get her to marry me, no big deal," Adam called from the living room. Both Kate and I laughed.

"I told you he'd get grouchy," I whispered.

We took the wine out to the guys. Kate sat next to Adam on the couch. A knock sounded at the door.

"I'll get it," I said.

"Hey," Emma said, walking through the door. "I brought tequila!" She hugged me quickly and I was shocked at how cold she was.

"Did you walk here?"

"Not far," she shrugged and we headed for the living room.

"Emma, nice to finally see you," Adam said gruffly.

"Oh, stop moping, I'm here and I've missed you too, so don't go all big brother ball buster on me." She put the liquor on the coffee table and hugged Adam, then Kate and Preston. "I was just telling Preston about the time you took me dress shopping, Em," Kate said. "She's great at picking stuff out."

Kate had come out of her shell so much since I saw her last. And I knew Adam was a credit to that. She was never an overly girly type of girl. Simple, plain and functional was her main criteria for most fashion. But just the fact that her hair was pinned back was a huge step of improvement. She always wore her long red mane completely down to cover the scars running from her jaw to her neck. Seeing the glow on her skin and happiness in her eyes, I wanted to hug Adam all over again for supporting Kate the way he has.

"Which reminds me, we have to go dress shopping for your bridesmaids' gowns."

Emma smiled. "Glad I brought the tequila then."

"It won't be that bad," I smiled. Emma may be a tough chick, but she had a frilly side—so long as it wasn't overdone. So naturally I had to mess with her a little. "I was thinking 'Gone With The Wind' theme. Head-to-toe lace and corsets."

"Ooh! And a mini-umbrella thing! What are those called?" Kate asked.

"Parasols," Emma grumbled.

"Yes! Those things are adorable." Kate said.

I laughed and Preston leaned over to say to Adam, "This is what you're in for, my friend."

Adam nodded. "I just need my fiancé to set a date. How did you get Megan on board so quick?"

17

●●●●●●●

"Oh my goodness!" Kate clamped her hand over her mouth. "Megan…you look so…"

I glanced down the front of me, then back at my best friends. Kate and Emma were sitting on two chairs facing me.

After lasagna night a couple weeks ago, Adam and Kate had headed back to Chicago and Emma had been scarce herself lately. We three girls hadn't got a chance to really catch up for a while.

Spot lighting drenched me in a soft yellow glow and I looked over my shoulder at the wall-sized mirror behind me. The seamstress fussed with the back of my dress as I stood there before the girls, waiting for their thoughts.

Kate fanned her eyes and Emma smiled wide.

"You look amazing, Megan!" Emma said, nearly bouncing out of her seat.

"It's perfect, Meg," Kate said, choking back a sob.

"Don't do that." I pointed at her. "Because you're going to make me cry if you start crying."

"I can't help it, I just…I'm just so happy for you."

The seamstress tugged on the dress, wrenching the breath from my chest. It was two days before the wedding and this was the final fitting. I swear this dress felt tighter than it did a few weeks ago.

"I'm sorry your mom can't be here," Kate said. She held up her cell phone and clicked a photo.

"Yeah, my dad isn't doing so well so they're coming in tomorrow for just the party and wedding."

"Is the new live-in nurse helping?" Emma asked.

I nodded. "*So* much. My mom said my dad is acclimating well with her and the help is wonderful."

"That's great!" Kate said.

The seamstress tugged again and an agonized groan pieced my lips. I sucked in harder, hoping this damn thing would fit.

"Did everything finally get squared away with Simon? Do you have custody?"

Kate sighed. "Not yet. His grandparents still legally have him but we get to see him all the time. Most of the week he stays at our place. I just want Tim to sign the damn papers."

"That guy is an ass-hat," Emma said, leaning back in her chair.

"Total ass-hat," Kate agreed. "Even in jail he has parental rights and is throwing fits about wanting his parents to take Simon. It's not that they don't want to, they are just getting older and it's hard chasing a little boy around. I've spoke with them and they aren't going to fight me trying to get full custody."

I nodded. "Well, Simon wants to be with you anyway, right?"

"Yeah." Kate looked down at her hands. "I want him so much. Adam is amazing with him and Simon just loves him to death. I just can't wait for this to really be over."

Emma patted Kate's shoulder.

"Things will work out," Kate affirmed, as if giving herself a mental pep talk. She ran her gaze along my dress again and smiled at me. "You look really happy, Megan. After everything that's happened..." she trailed off and I knew where she was going with it.

"I am happy." And that was the truth. What started out as a contract ended up being more. A small grin tugged at my lips when I recited the same thought I'd been having for over a month: I was in love with John Preston Strauss.

Though I hadn't said it to him yet, I was confident the rules of the game had changed that night he came for me in my apartment. Every day he opened up a bit more. Between planning the wedding and a nearly insatiable fiancé, my days and nights had been pretty booked, but I was so glad I finally had my two friends in the same room, and that this wedding was actually happening.

"Well, anyone can see how much he adores you," Emma said. We had all spent the last couple days together. Both Adam and Kate were in a suite at the hotel. We'd all been nearly inseparable. Dinners and lunches. Planning the final touches on the wedding. I was so grateful that Adam and Kate were able to fly in a few days early.

"Well, I swear Adam has a man crush on Preston, he won't shut up about him," Kate said.

"Tell me about it."

Preston talked about Adam too. They had a lot in common, being business moguls and whatnot. I wanted to roll my eyes a little, but it was good Preston had made a friend out of Adam. He had only spoken of one other man, Rhys, who I met at the Armory event. He was showing up for the wedding—a fact Emma avoided like the plague so I didn't push her on it.

"Adam said that Preston has a hotel in Chicago. Any chance you might be coming back home to set up shop?" Kate's eyes sparkled, and I couldn't help but love the idea too.

Preston has said we'd look for a house after the wedding. Chicago was near Kate and my parents. And Emma would go back there eventually, I hoped. Like Rhys, it was a touchy subject and every time Adam approached her with coming home, Emma tensed up.

"That would be pretty awesome."

"Come on girls, your turn." A plump little woman in her sixties clapped her hands at Emma and Kate. "Time to see how you look in your bridesmaids' dresses."

"Make sure you come show me!" I said.

"Duh," Emma called back and winked. "Thank God you ditched the parasol idea."

"It's not too late to get them," I called after her.

I had my two friends in my wedding, my father was getting the health care he needed and my parents wouldn't lose their home. And I was standing in a gown on the brink of marrying the one man I'd ever felt this insane about.

"I love him," I whispered.

No ifs. It was a fact. My stomach turned and I palmed my belly. Taking a deep breath, I willed away the heartburn I'd been dealing with over the past couple of weeks. Between the fast pace of all this planning and the inevitable stress, my body was suffering. I just hoped this little stomach bug went away before this weekend. I smiled. I told myself the same thing I had the past few weeks: It's nothing I can't handle—

Dizziness suddenly swept over me and I jerked forward, almost falling off the platform.

"Oh, dear, you alright?" The seamstress grabbed my arm and steadied me.

"Yeah," I swallowed, putting the back of my hand against my mouth. Nausea crept over me, leaving my skin feeling cool and sticky. I wanted to throw a fit because this was ridiculous—almost a month and these flu symptoms were still hanging around. "I just feel a bit dizzy."

She helped me sit down. "Poor thing. I know in my first trimester I was dizzy and sick all the time."

My eyes snapped to the woman. "Excuse me?"

She looked at me with shock and worry on her face. "Well… you're…you're pregnant, aren't you?"

I shook my head furiously. "No."

"Oh…" She looked at my stomach. "Are you sure?"

My mouth just hung open. I didn't know if I wanted to laugh or cry. Maybe feel insulted? I had been getting sick lately, but that was the bug. Right?

"I'm on the pill." I blurted out. It was the only thing that made sense that I could cling to in that moment.

"Well, maybe go chat with your doctor, because I don't mean to be rude, but I'm going to have to take your dress out a good inch. Unless you've been giving into a doughnut addiction?"

My skin was already cold but now the mist of sweat that broke made me freeze. Out of nowhere, a hot flash skated over me, drowning out the iciness in my veins and replacing it with fire. I was certain I would pass out. I mentally ran though the checklist of my symptoms the last several weeks: Nauseous, bloated, and my breasts hurt a little. Vomiting and dizzy spells.

"Oh God…"

18

"You don't look so good," a snotty voice said.

Stopping in the middle of The Strauss Hotel lobby, I looked up to find Darlene smiling at me. She, Charlie and John all lived in the city, but, "Why are you here?" My voice was flat and a cold sweat covered my entire body. Darlene was the last person I needed to see right now.

"Oh, I was just popping in to catch you actually." She glanced at her diamond-encrusted watch. "I thought you'd be done dress shopping a while ago. What happened? Make a detour?"

Her insinuating tone and smirk drained the little blood left in my face. She couldn't possibly know…could she? I had left the dress fitting early and Preston's driver took me straight to the doctor. Preston told me once not to put anything past Darlene. The fact that she knew my schedule was beyond unnerving.

"What do you want, Darlene?"

People shuffled around us in and out of the front doors. She stepped several paces to the closest corner, away from the bustling comers and goers. Part of me wanted to complete my mission and run upstairs to find Preston instead of deal with her right now. But again, that evil grin splitting her face had me uneasy.

I moved to her. "What?" I snapped.

"So moody." She glanced at my stomach. My pulse raced and those dizzy spells I had been having kicked into high gear. Standing upright was taking the majority of my focus.

"You shouldn't be so testy with me when I came here to give you a friendly heads up."

I shook my head.

"John is waiting for you in the office upstairs."

I glanced at the elevator.

"Oh, don't worry," she examined her nails, "Preston isn't here."

"Whatever reason you've found to take a personal interest in mine and my fiancé's schedule needs to stop. We're getting married and you need to accept that."

"Are you?" She nearly giggled with glee. "Well, I suppose you must be getting married since that is what the whole contract entails."

My stomach bottomed out and a fresh flash of cold coated my bones.

"I knew you two were up to something. I just didn't think Preston had to buy his women now." She scoffed. "I guess that's what fishing for losers with a bad history will get you." Her eyes trailed the entire length of me, and if looks could kill, hers would maim. "You settled pretty cheap, don't you think? Only five million? Needless to say John was very upset when I told him and gave him a copy of the contract."

She tilted her head and glanced at my belly again. "Not that any of it matters now." No woman had ever smiled as big as Darlene did in that moment.

The world was spinning way too fast, and I couldn't get a grip. Couldn't get my feet to completely touch the ground. Couldn't even muster words to fight back. My mind was spent, terror and uncertainty had already been circling, but now blood-chilling fear that I was on the brink of losing everything I held dear was crashing down.

When her leer didn't leave my waistline, a spark of raw ferocity boiled over in my chest.

"You are a sad, disgusting woman." I stepped closer. "Don't ever come near me or Preston again."

She blinked rapidly as if shocked I had spoken. Her throat worked hard on a swallow and she straightened her stance like my words literally knocked her down a peg.

"You really think he's going to keep you after he finds out you lost the deal for him?" Her smirk was back in place.

"He loves me," I growled. Though he'd never said it, in that moment, I knew that to be true. It had to be. While the words didn't come out, everyday *loved* was what he made me feel.

Darlene plucked her sunglasses out of her purse and put them on. Walking past me, she brushed my shoulder and mumbled, "We'll see about that."

● ● ●

John was pacing in front of the large desk in the office. When he heard me walk in and shut the door, he swung around and faced me.

"Is this true?" he asked, and pointed at the contract on the desk. The poor man looked genuinely hurt and confused. He broad shoulders were slightly sunken and his normally sparkly eyes dimmed. Now was a time I really needed Preston, and after three calls and only getting his voicemail, I was in this on my own for the time being.

"Yes," I whispered.

He folded his arms over his chest—not in an angry way, but in a way that looked like he was giving himself a hug.

"John, I'm sorry I lied to you. Things between Preston and I did start off with that." I lifted my chin at the contract. "But," I closed the distance between us and looked him in the eyes.

"Please believe me now when I say that I love your son more than anything."

He let out a loud breath and gently cupped my shoulders. Then, he did the most unexpected thing, he pulled me into a hug.

"Oh, child, I know you do." His voice was soothing and the tears I'd been fighting all afternoon broke out. I hugged him back, feeling so lost, so scared, so unsure.

He ran one palm over the back of my head, softly stroking my hair. My father used to do the same thing when I was a little girl and the comforting action made me sob a little harder.

"I never meant to drive him to this. Having a family, children of your own, is something I've always valued. After Preston's mother died, he took on the world by himself, never relying on or wanting anyone else. And that's my fault." He slowly pulled back and looked at me. "Preston has been through a lot in his life, but I've never seen him look at someone the way he does you."

A small watery smile tugged at my lips.

"I just want him to be happy. I never meant to hurt you or deceive you."

"I know that too. Which is why I'm leaving this up to you two. I meant what I said, I'm giving him the three percent as a wedding gift." He cupped my cheek and sadness marred his face. "If the wedding still happens on Saturday."

My breath hitched. It was a fear I'd been having all day. I didn't know how much John knew and what exactly Darlene had said, but I had my own discussion with Preston to worry about.

"Have you spoken to Preston about this?"

John shook his head. "No. But I would assume that Darlene has found a way to tell him by now."

That wouldn't be surprising.

"I'd be so proud to have you in our family," John said and the sweet tone that laced his words forced me to believe him.

"Thank you."

My knees shook and my face was flickering between hot and cold. John believed in Preston and me. I could only hope his son felt the same way.

19

"Jesus Christ," Preston said, slamming the door.

I was curled up on the couch in our penthouse. He sat next to me and rubbed my shoulder.

"I take it you know about Darlene and the contract?"

"Short of breaking and entering, I have no idea how she got her hands on it." My money was on the sneaking and thieving explanation. "I spoke with my father on the way home, everything will be fine. We're still getting married and this whole thing won't matter."

"It matters to me," I whispered. I drew my knees up to my stomach and hugged them. "I'm tired of being a contract, Preston."

He frowned.

He was obviously on the frazzled side but dealt with it well. A blow like this out of nowhere could do that, but Preston looked pretty collected, as if he always had a backup plan.

"Is there something else going on, Megan?" His tone was a bit gravelly. He was examining my face like I was some kind of suspect.

"Yeah." I glanced at my hands. "There is."

I took a deep breath and looked him in the eye, which was difficult because as soon as I did, mine started buzzing like angry hornets had set up a hive behind my retinas. He looked so worried. About me.

Another deep breath.

The last couple hours had been hell. All kinds of thoughts and scenarios were playing through my head. Shock didn't begin to describe the state I was in—and had been in since this afternoon. But somehow, with those green eyes glaring back at me, I felt a little better. Like everything would be okay. It *had* to be okay.

This wasn't two months ago. This was now. I loved Preston. And somewhere deep down, I believed he loved me. The contract wasn't a forefront fixture in our relationship anymore.

"What we have…it's real…right?"

"Yes. This is real, sweetheart," Preston said and rubbed my shin. For the first time in the last few hours a surge of happiness raced through me and beat all the doom out of my head.

Clinging to his words, I told him the truth.

"I'm pregnant."

Preston's face turned from concern to a mask of shock and finally, rage. My heart pounded in my ears and my chest felt too tight to hold my ribcage.

"What?" He stood and ran a hand through his hair. His glare licked over me like flames. There was so much hate and animosity seeping from him, it almost choked me. "How did you do this?"

"I didn't…I mean, I didn't purposefully—"

"Bullshit!" he yelled and I jumped in my seat at his outburst. "I check your birth control pills every evening."

"You what? You've been checking to see if I take them?"

"Yes. So what, you've been tossing them? Should have fucking known," he growled.

My entire chest completely hollowed out as if Preston's words grew claws and snatched the heart straight from between my ribs. Not a single word made sense. It couldn't be happening. Not this way. I knew this was a surprise but…

154

"I thought this was real? You just said that…You and I…"

"*You* are lying and conniving and *I* am not going to be trapped with this!"

I couldn't breathe. Couldn't even work my mouth closed and open to produce words. I wanted to tell him that I didn't mean for this to happen. Tell him what the doctor told me. Tell him that even though it was a shock, I was excited about this baby. Our baby. Anything to make him stop looking at me like I was evil incarnate. Unfortunately, I knew Preston, I knew how terrible his thoughts could be and now they were aimed at me.

The sickness I'd felt over the last several weeks was nothing compared to the present churning in my gut. It didn't matter what my defense was. Reality, love—I shook my head. I'd been naïve. Jumping straight to blame and horror was a clear expression of exactly how he really felt about me. His reaction was more than enough. And it was too much to bear.

"You may think you're getting away with something, but you won't get a thing from me."

"I don't want anything from you," I whispered.

He scoffed, obviously not believing me.

I stood up, my legs shaky and all my will gone. I was tired. So unbelievingly tired I could barely see. Tears danced on the rim of my eyes. The only thing that came to mind was the truth.

"I love you, Preston."

And my heart broke because it didn't matter. The look on his face made that clear. "It's true," I said. "But I don't think I've ever hated someone this much in my life."

I bit my lip because the tears came down hard. I couldn't look at him anymore. My chest was caving in and my lungs were burning. There wasn't enough oxygen in the world at the moment. I turned and walked to the door.

"I thought you were different," he growled.

I looked over my shoulder and opened the door. "So did I."

20

"We'll figure it out. Don't worry, Meg."

I sat on Kate's bed while she hugged and rocked me. I would have gone back to my apartment but didn't think I could make it. Once the penthouse door shut behind me, I'd broken down. Kate and Adam's suite was only an elevator ride away.

I sniffled. "I'm so sorry, I didn't mean to barge in on you."

Kate shook her head. "Don't you be sorry. You just worry about you right now, Meg. I'm here. Everything will be okay."

I had cried all night and the words I so desperately needed to hear came from my best friend instead of the man I was in love with…the man whose child I was carrying.

"It hurts," I breathed.

It was the same thing I told my mother with a smile a month ago. I loved him so much it hurt. She told me it was the best kind. But right then, I didn't see how that was possible. Gravity was pushing against me and my bones were slowly cracking under the pressure and digging into my muscles. I was suffocating and my body caving in around itself. Pain. Total and utter pain.

"I know it does," she whispered.

It was well past four in the morning and Kate had cried with me all night. Adam was pacing by the bedroom doorway, occasionally stopping to glower. At first I thought he was mad at me, but soon realized he was upset with Preston.

"Here you go," Adam said, and set two cups of tea on the nightstand.

"Thanks, Adam."

He nodded and before he left said, "Men can be really stupid."

His blue eyes landed on Kate and I knew what he was talking about. Several months ago he had almost lost her and the look on his face showed he still hadn't forgiven himself.

"Why didn't you tell Preston what the doctor said?" Kate asked softly. "That when you took the antibiotics for your ear, it messed with your birth control. Why did you just let him blame you?"

"It doesn't matter. His first reaction was hate and denial." Holding desperately to my control, I forced myself to keep the sobbing at bay. "I honestly thought he loved me."

"He does!" Kate hugged me tight. "He wouldn't have proposed if he didn't."

I looked at her and all the control on the planet couldn't keep the tears from starting up again. "It wasn't real."

She frowned. "What do you mean?"

"It was fake, all of it. I needed the money and he needed a wife," I began and over the next hour I told Kate every humiliating detail—from the first night, to the contract, to the money, to my parents' losing everything. It didn't matter anymore. Preston had said that pregnancy voids everything. The contract wasn't valid anymore.

"Oh, Meg…"

"It's stupid, I know."

"No, no it's not. You're a good person, an amazing daughter and what happened in Chicago with Tim was not your fault. You have to stop blaming yourself for that."

I shook my head. I was so lost. So far beyond lost. Sadness drowned me like frozen lake water and I couldn't catch my breath. Bone-chilling cold seeped from every pore and I didn't think I'd ever feel true warmth again.

"I just…I thought Preston was different. I know he has some issues but I've been honest with him."

"What are you going to do?"

"I don't know." I wiped my eyes and put a palm to my stomach. "But I want this baby."

Kate nodded.

I wouldn't go after Preston for anything. Not a dime, not his name, not anything. But this little thing inside me was mine. Something innocent and good, and I wouldn't take that for granted.

Kate's phone buzzed on the bedside table. She reached for it.

"Hello?" Kate frowned at me. "Hi, Judy. Yeah she's right here."

My heart stilled and I took the phone. "Mom?"

"I tried calling your p-phone but it went straight to voicemail and I know K-Kate was visiting…"

My mother was on crying and on the brink of hysteria. Damn it! I'd left my phone at the penthouse along with everything else. "Mom, it's okay. What's going on?"

"Your dad is m-missing."

Dread and terror wrecked into me like a one-ton anvil. It was everything I could do to pull myself together and not vomit.

"What happened?"

"I don't know. I woke up because I heard a banging sound. The front door was wide open and your father was g-gone."

"It's okay, mom," I whispered, not sure at all if it really was.

"If he's confused and wandering around lost—" a sob broke my mother's voice and I clamped a hand around my own mouth to keep from doing the same thing.

"We'll find him. I want you to hang up with me, and call the police. I'm going to the airport now." I shot up and Kate followed suit, worry plaguing her face. She went to the closet and grabbed her coat. "I'm on the next flight home. You stay there, call the police and wait for them, okay?"

"O-okay." I'd never heard my poor mother so scared in my whole life.

"Call me on Kate's phone if you need, but as soon as I get on the plane I'll let you know."

"Thank you."

The phone clicked off and I grabbed my shoes.

"What's going on?" Kate asked.

"My dad is missing. I think he wandered off and," I choked then cleared my throat, "I have to go."

"Of course!" Kate called for Adam and in less than two minutes he had a car waiting out front of the hotel.

"I don't have my I.D. or any money—"

"Don't worry about it," Adam said, stuffing his cell in his pocket. "I have it covered. We're taking a private plane out of here, it'll be ready by the time we get to the airport."

Tears ran down my cheeks but I smiled at him. "Thank you so much."

He wrapped one of Kate's coats around me. "You're family, Megan."

Kate nodded and put her arm around me, picking up her purse as we walked toward the front door and out.

"Everything will be okay," Kate whispered, rubbing my shoulder. I looked at her and hopped to God she was right. Because I didn't think I could handle losing one more thing I loved.

21

Beep…beep…beep…

I clutched my father's hand and stared at the heart monitor.

"Why don't you come with me to the cafeteria, honey," my mom asked. She looked fragile, as though she'd aged ten years in the past ten hours. "That's okay. I want to stay with him." By the time I had gotten back home, the police had found him shivering on a park bench about a mile from my parents' house. When he first woke up in the hospital, he was disoriented and scared but relatively aware. The doctors got him calm and he was now sleeping.

"The doctors said he should be cleared to go home tonight."

I nodded. They had hooked him up to an I.V. drip for hydration and ran several tests to make sure he hadn't suffered any strokes. Everything came back clear. They think that he woke up confused and wandered off on his own, which was apparently not uncommon for dementia patients.

"I was going to ask them if we could still travel for your wedding tomorrow."

"No, mom. I don't want to push him. And…the wedding…" I gripped my father's hand a little tighter.

"He wouldn't want you postpone, honey. Have you called Preston? I'm sure he's worried sick—"

"I'm sorry, mom, but do mind if I just have a few minutes?" Adrenaline was crashing and every emotion known to man was pulsing on and off within me like a spastic child flicking a light switch. I hadn't brought myself to admit anything to my mother yet.

"Of course. I'll bring you back some coffee, okay?"

"Thanks."

With a pat on my shoulder, her soft footsteps faded from the room, leaving me alone with my sleeping father.

"Daddy," I whispered, and hung my head. "I'm so scared."

Tears ran down my face and hit the top of his hand I was holding. He looked older since I saw him last. Smaller. I felt helpless and didn't even know where to begin sorting any of this out. For now, I focused on the positive things. He was alive and okay. And hopefully, he'd wake up and be relatively cognizant.

A warm palm ran down my back. I turned to find—

"Preston?" My voice held almost no sound. A tidal wave of warmth and relief crashed over me, then was quickly sucked up by an empty funnel of frost. Emotions warred and I didn't know how to feel.

"I'm sorry, Megan." He glanced at my father. "Is he going to be okay?"

"Yes." I stood to face him, using the edge of the bed to balance my weak legs and tugged on my shirt near my belly button. His eyes flew to the action and something terrified and painful flashed across his face.

"Are you okay?"

I wanted to balk. How could he ask me that? "No."

"Please, sweetheart…" he mumbled just loud enough to reach my ears. He reached out for me and I stepped back.

"Fuck…" he whispered, and halted. "I lost you, didn't I?"

I didn't speak. Couldn't. After a night of crying and sick with worry, I wasn't prepared to take him on. What I needed to say was stuck in my throat. Tears coated every syllable I attempted, and I began to choke on my words before they even left my mouth.

"I have nothing, sweetheart." He stepped again, and again I moved back. "I have nothing to offer you, to show you, prove to you that I deserve you. Because I don't."

I bit my bottom lip but the damn thing trembled anyway. There had to be some strength left in me, I just needed to find it. Tell him that I was keeping the baby whether he liked it or not. Tell him that I didn't need him, but just the thought going through my mind brought a fresh dose of gut-wrenching pain.

He stared hard at my face. "I tried to find you. When I learned about your father, I came here." He ran a hand through his hair and his red-rimmed eyes glanced at the ceiling. "I've tried making sense of this all night. I've pored over documents, bank statements, bills and I found nothing."

I frowned. Not understanding where he was going with this.

He apparently caught on to my confusion because he explained, "You have access to a lot. Money, credit, the Strauss name, and you didn't use any of it. The weekly allowance I gave you was directly wired every Monday to your parents and that's it."

He was saying things I already knew, but obviously he had thought something very different about me. "Did you really think I would use you like that? It's never been about the money, not in the way you're implying."

"I know what it's been about. Because that's what I made it about," he whispered. Not blaming, just stating. "And I made you feel like you couldn't come to me. I'll never forgive myself for not being there for you last night, Megan. Not being the one you turned to when you found out about your father, because I pushed you away when you needed me most."

A humorless laugh escaped his mouth and all I could do was stand mute, my heart breaking.

"I knew better," he said. "The contract was meant to keep all of these kinds of things at bay. No mess. No emotions. You were supposed to be an element I controlled within my world."

My head hung and my pulse pounded through my temples. He must have taken the opportunity to move closer when I wasn't looking because I felt his heat surround me, chasing that nagging chill away. Then he did the most unexpected thing—he hit his knees before me.

"Megan, *you* are my world."

He looked so defeated, so sad. His hands fisted in his lap, as if trying not to reach out for me.

"I don't know how or when it happened. But it did. You. Are. Everything." His voice cracked just enough to send a sharp sting of pain racing through my blood.

I shook my head. It hurt. All of this hurt too much. "Preston… you can't just…"

I stepped back and his hands shot out and grabbed the back of my thighs.

"No, no don't do that," his plea was so low I could barely hear it. I'd never seen such pure fear mar a man's face. "I'm sorry, sweetheart. So, so sorry. I can't. I can't lose you." He pulled me close and wrapped his arms around my waist and pressed his face against my stomach.

"Either of you," he whispered.

Tears fell so hard I couldn't stop it. Large drops tracked down my face and plummeted onto the top of his head.

"I love you, Megan." His arms encased me harder. "Whatever it takes to prove that to you, I will do. There's so much I'm not ready for. Not good at…but I'll try."

"I just wanted to make you happy. Give you, help you get, everything you wanted," I whispered. "I didn't get pregnant on purpose."

His breath fanned over my belly on a long exhale. "I know. And what I want is you."

"Why?" I whispered, more defeat washing over me. "I can't help you anymore. Your father made it clear that if you don't get married tomorrow, you won't get the three percent."

That must be the reason he came back, to talk me into leaving today and the wedding—

"I don't care about the three percent." He buried his face in my stomach and splayed his fingers over my lower back. "I don't care if I lose the whole empire. All I care about is you. Our baby. Our family. Your father is important and I'm staying here until he's well."

"Meg-Pie?" My father's sleepy voice called out from behind me.

Preston rose to his feet and I spun to face him.

"I'm here, Daddy."

He smiled and his eyes opened further, looking at me, then Preston.

"And who is this young man?"

I glanced at Preston. "That's the man I'm in love with."

My father smiled and raised his hand to Preston. He clasped it gently and shook. "Sir."

"Well," he sat up slightly in bed and I gripped his forearm. "You're as fussy as your mother," he playfully growled at me. "Let me sit up here so I can look at the boy." He looked at Preston for a long moment then at me. "This is the one you're set to marry?"

I opened my mouth to speak, but Preston jumped in.

"If she'll have me, sir." Preston reached for my hand and I let him. Twining our fingers he whispered in my ear, "I'll wait as long as it takes. Do whatever you command. But understand that I'm not letting you go."

"Well, that sounds like a man who is worthy," my father chuckled.

I laughed a little and Preston took me in his arms and kissed every last ounce of pain away. Hugging him tight, I pulled him as close as I could.

"I love you," he whispered against my mouth.

"I love you too."

"I'm glad." He smiled. "Because we both know I'm not above bribery."

22

"You look beautiful, Meg-pie."

I clutched to my father's arm and smiled up at him. "Thank you, Daddy."

The violin started playing, our cue. My dad gently cleared his throat, which sounded more like a low sob, and looked down at me. There was a misty sparkle in his blue eyes. Recognition.

It had been a few weeks since he woke up in the hospital, and since then, he was having more good days than bad. Something I was beyond grateful for.

"I don't care what is happening today," he said. "You will always be my baby girl."

Batting my lashes against the rising tears, I nodded. Right now, my father knew who I was, and in that first step down the aisle, he was walking me toward the man I loved. This moment was the one I had thought of from the time I was a little girl. This was the moment I clung to when everything else seemed lost.

It was a moment of clarity.

I was walking toward a promise of something better. Something real. And that promise was in a crisp black tuxedo with the most hypnotic green eyes. Preston's gaze never left mine as my father took me closer and closer to the altar.

In that moment, everything was perfect.

● ● ●

"Please God don't make me do the funky chicken again," Emma groaned.

Kate and I just laughed. We had taken a break from dancing and sat at the table. The reception had been in full swing for hours and everyone seemed to be enjoying themselves. Charlie and Darlene didn't bother showing up to either the wedding or reception, which was fine with me. Despite having to push the date back a few weeks, many of our guests still made it.

I looked around and took in every sight and sound of the magic in the room. My parents were dancing together and the smile on my mother's face made me light up inside. Across the room, a pair of dark emerald eyes watched me. Even at a distance, I could feel Preston's heat snare me.

"Is it just me, or does the man look even sexier with a wedding band on his finger?" I sighed, openly ogling my husband.

Husband. The word would take some getting used to. But it was definitely growing on me.

"I think Emma is more taken with the guy Preston's talking to," Kate teased, elbowing Emma's side.

"Please," Emma said and took a long swallow of champagne. "I'm not taken with anyone."

"Oh, I think you are," Kate said. "Who is that anyway?"

"That's Preston's friend, Rhys Striker. Emma, you've met Rhys." I wiggled my brows at her.

She had been acting more and more flighty lately and never once spoke about Rhys since the night of the Armory. But the way they were staring at each other meant obviously something was going on there. Other than him formerly being in the military and a part of the millionaire club, I didn't know much about him.

Emma's gaze skated back to Rhys and I hid a grin. Just when I thought I saw a spark of interest in Emma's eye, and hoped that she'd admit to whatever was going on with this guy, she glanced away mumbling something along the lines of Rhys looking like Thor. I didn't really hear her because Preston was closing in on me, and the man made everything else melt away when he came near.

"Mrs. Strauss," he said, and held out his hand. "May I have this dance?"

My face already hurt from the amount of smiling I'd been doing, but at this rate, I'd never be able to stop. I was so beyond happy that life just seemed simple.

"Of course."

Preston helped me to my feet just as the band began slowing the rhythm. Walking to the middle of the floor, Preston pulled me into his strong arms and swayed me effortlessly.

"Have I told you how beautiful you look?"

"Only about a thousand times." I went up on my tiptoes and kissed him.

"I've been thinking." He spun me then brought me back. "I want to put the three percent my father gave us in our child's name."

My mouth hung open. Though we hadn't kept the original wedding date, John still gave his shares to Preston and was elated to find out we were expecting.

"It's you're company—"

"It's *ours*," he said, squeezing my right hand.

"What do you think of naming him Leo?" he asked.

"My dad?"

Preston grinned. "Sort of. I was thinking if it's a boy…" Cupping my hip, his thumb rubbed across my stomach. "We could name him Leopold after your father."

I didn't think it was possible for my eyes to produce any more tears that day, but sure enough, they started flooding again.

"I like it. Leopold Preston Strauss."

Preston's jaw clenched and so much happiness rippled off him.

"I'm so in love with you," I murmured.

"And I'm beyond a rational thought in love with you, sweetheart."

In the middle of the glossy dance floor, locked in Preston's arms, I realized that he never had the power to drown out the world around me. He *was* the force that my entire universe spun around.

"I'm going to make you happy, Megan."

I looked up at the man who started out as a wild one-nighter, then became a contract lover, only to end up changing the rules and possessing me completely.

"I believe you."

The End

But...

Turn the page for some bonus material!

ADAM AND KATE

"I've been waiting all damn night to get you out of this dress," Adam said, trailing his mouth from my lips to my jaw. He blindly opened our suite door while I frantically unbuttoned his shirt. We had just seen Preston and Megan off for their honeymoon and didn't even make it out of the elevator before we were undressing at each other.

"Marry me," he said, kicking the door shut behind him and backing me into the room.

"Yes," I whispered, continuing to kiss him like crazy. That was the main feeling Adam brought out in me. Crazy. A few months ago that scared me. Now, I loved it. He was my anchor, just as much as he was my wings.

Every day he asked me to marry him, and every day I said yes. What he was really asking would be the question that came next. The same question he'd been asking since he proposed.

"When?" He unzipped my short strapless dress and shoved it down leaving me in nothing but my panties.

I kicked off my high heels.

"Fuck, baby," he growled, cupping my breasts, gently pushing me to sit down on the edge of the bed.

He stood and finished removing his shirt. His eyes were fixated between my legs and he lifted his chin. "Spread those pretty legs."

I did. He tore at his belt and shed the rest of his clothes in one quick movement.

"Wider," he barked.

Hitting his knees before me, he scooted between my thighs. He was eye level with my breasts, and with hands splayed over my back, he brought me closer and snaked his tongue over one aching nipple. I moaned and drove my fingers into his hair.

"You taste so good. I don't think I'll ever get enough of you." He sucked the rosy peak hard and I arched into him. "You like that?"

I nodded, tightening my grip on the silky strands of his hair.

"What about this?" He circled his tongue around the throbbing bud, lightly teasing and causing my skin to heat and prickle.

"Yes," I breathed, tugging him closer.

"Oh, you want more?"

"More. Harder..." I pushed my breast farther into his mouth.

"You asked for it." He bit down on my nipple. A flash of wetness rushed to my pussy. He had me on the edge of coming already.

"Yes!" I gasped. Placing my hands behind me, I leaned back and let him devour me. Only Adam could play my body so well and have me begging for release without even touching below the waist. I felt empty—needed to show him all the passion I was feeling.

"I want to taste you," I moaned.

He looked up at me and I sat up straight, opening my mouth.

"God damn it you're gorgeous," he growled and rose.

He stood between my spread thighs and guided his hard cock between my lips. Keeping my gaze on his, I licked all around the crown, then down the length, and back up again.

He muttered a curse.

"Let me do all the work," I said. Then with a small smile and final flick of my tongue on the tip, I swallowed him whole.

"Ah—Kate!" His muscles trembled in efforts to keep still while I bobbed up and down, impaling my mouth on him over and over. A low rumble broke from his throat and he gripped my shoulders and gently pushed me away.

"You're distracting me," he rasped and hit his knees once more. "I want to know *when*, Kate."

He bit my inner thigh then tore my panties away. The sound of lace ripping echoed in the dark room. His breath was hot against my core and I tried rocking my hips, coaxing him to make contact, but he didn't let me.

"When?" he asked again, terser this time.

"Soon," I breathed.

Hands on either side of my lap, I gripped the bedding and wiggled my way closer to him, desperately trying to get him to taste me where I wanted most. But he just subtly moved his head and nipped my other thigh.

"You love me," he stated, the words delivering a puff of air against my hot flesh.

"So much," I said.

His tongue snapped out, quickly tapping my clit and I gasped. "And you're wet for me."

"All the time," I agreed.

Tap.

"Yet you won't marry me."

"I will!"

He sank his tongue inside and I cried out in ecstasy. He delved in and out mercilessly. Throwing my head back, I pushed my hips out to meet every thrust of his amazing tongue.

"When?" he growled again. Trading off between licking my clit then diving back inside was torture. He was purposefully keeping me right on the brink, not allowing me to go over.

"Please Adam," I begged. My skin was on fire, my veins ready to burst from the pleasure. I loved this man. He was what made sense in my world. What I clung to. What I fought for. He was everything and then, all I wanted was to feel him.

I clawed at his shoulders and scooted up the bed. Lying completely back, I tugged on his arm and he followed me, crawling up my body and cradling himself between my thighs. His hard cock prodded at my entrance and I reached between us to grip him and guide him inside my body.

We sighed in unison. Happy to be connected, because nothing felt so right. My world was complete when he was a part of me.

"Katelyn," he whispered. Balancing his weight one hand, he cupped my cheek in the other. Slowly rocking his hips, in and out, he kept that ice-blue gaze on me, and slowly rubbed my cheekbone.

His hard chest ran along my sensitive breasts, swollen from his attentions earlier. His skin against mine sparked my nerve like lightning to a lake. Raw energy bubbled beneath the surface and static lust prickled every cell. He retreated so far that only the crown rimmed my opening, then thrust forward, long and hard. Steady and intense. Watching intently as he slowly pushed me over the edge.

Snaking one arm underneath me, his body made full contact with mine, not an ounce of his weight spared. He hugged me close. The power of his hold was almost crushing, suffocating, but I was desperate for more. I wanted to drown in him. Be taken over completely. With every thrust, he delivered dose after dose of pleasure. I let go, trusting him to hang on to me. He wouldn't let me fall too far and he wouldn't let go.

Locking my legs around his back I clutched him as tightly as I could. He stayed buried deep within me, circling and stirring, hitting that sensitive spot inside again and again without putting an inch of space between us. No matter where I went or what happened, this—Adam—was my home. My salvation.

"Now," I whispered.

Pleasure shot through me like a bullet, ripping through my limbs, leaving goose bumps in its wake. Gritting my teeth, I sobbed from the ferocity of my orgasm, spurred on when Adam came, his hot release surging over and over.

Breathing hard, Adam rose up enough to look me in the eyes. I cupped his face in my palms and between gasps for air and a wide smile on my face, I said, "Now. I want to marry you *right now.*"

● ● ●

Several calls, one marriage license and a set of "I do's" later, I was officially Mrs. Adam Kinkade. Staring out at the clear blue ocean, I watched the sun slowly rise off the coast of Hawaii.

"It's been a long few days, baby. Come back to bed," Adam said, walking up behind me. He wrapped his strong arms around my middle and I snuggled into his warmth. With his chin on my shoulder, we both stared at the expanse of water before us, listening to the faintest sounds of waves lapping.

"This is what peace feels like, isn't it?" I turned my neck enough to face him. He kissed me softly on the lips and like every other time—and likely every time to come for the rest of my life—I melted.

"*You* are my peace," he said. "Thank you." His tone was so quiet, so loving, it brought tears to my eyes. "I know you wanted things to be better and for us to have Simon before we got married, but I promise you, baby," he kissed me again, "I will make that happen."

I nodded, because I believed him. Yes, I did want things "better" and I wanted Simon legally. But I wanted Adam too. After seeing my best friend go through what she did, almost lose the man she loved, watching them join their lives together just made sense. I trusted Adam. Everything would be okay. It had to be.

"Do you have regrets?" he asked.

I frowned. "What?"

His body tensed a little around me. "I didn't give you the big wedding you deserved."

I laughed. "I just wanted you. Besides—" I turned within his arms and faced him. "Whisking me away to Kauai and getting a private piece of the island all to ourselves is not a bad way to tie the knot."

"We can still have a wedding. A reception. Anything you want."

I rested my forehead against his chest. "I just want our lives to finally start."

Tucking a finger under my chin, he raised my gaze to his. "Mine did, the day I met you."

The tears I was fighting broke free. "I love you so much."

"I love you, wife." A wide grin split his face and for the rest of my days I didn't think I'd ever get used to the shockingly sexy sight of Adam Kinkade smiling.

● ● ●

After a few days in New York and then Hawaii, I was excited to get back to Chicago. It was nice spending time alone with Adam, but he spent a good chunk of time on the phone in private.

"I have one more surprise for you," Adam said as the elevator opened to our apartment.

"Kate!" A small voice came from around the corner. Running down the hall and barreling right toward me was Simon.

"Oh, buddy!" I dropped to my knees and caught him in a big hug. "I missed you so much."

"I missed you too." He squeezed my neck. "Grandma and Grandpa said I get to live with you now."

I looked at Adam, then saw Tim's parents, Shelia and Hank, walk into view smiling.

"I'm sorry I've been preoccupied and on the phone a lot the last few days, but," Adam looked at Simon, "I've been working some stuff out." His eyes were luminous beacons staring down at me. "Tim signed the papers, love."

My eyes went wide and I hugged Simon closer. "R-really?"

He nodded. "We have temporary full custody. The social worker will be here to check things out next week. Once that's all squared away, Simon is ours."

Tears streamed down my cheeks. All I could say was thank you. Over and over. Adam ruffled Simon's hair and I stood. Surrounded by my two men, my life was finally coming together.

"Everything really is going to be okay?" I looked up at the man with the fierce blue eyes that changed my life with one look.

"Yes." The promise in his deep voice was all the proof I needed that the world finally made sense, and maybe didn't hurt the way I once thought it did.

"Hello, dear," Shelia said, and gave me a hug.

"Hi, Sheila how are you two doing?" Though Tim was a sad-sack, his parents were actually really great. They've been nothing but supportive through this whole process.

"We're good," Sheila said. "That guy of yours sure knows how to make things happen."

I smiled and looked over my shoulder at Adam. "Yes he does."

Sheila shook her head, her gray crop cut shuffling along her brow. "I just couldn't believe it. All the phone calls and work he put in. He really loves you and Simon."

I never doubted that for a moment. In the middle of Sheila catching me up on the last week's events, Adam's cell rang and he took the call, mumbling something I couldn't understand near the corner of the room.

"Can I go play in my room?" Simon asked. We had a room set up for him complete with toys and decked out in dinosaurs décor since I moved in with Adam last year.

"Of course, sweetie."

Simon ran to his bedroom and I glanced back at Adam. A stern look crossed his face and he jammed his phone into his pocket.

"Is everything okay?" I asked him.

He ran a hand through his hair, shaking his head. "Emma's in trouble."

● ● ●

*Look for **Seduce Me Slowly**, Emma's book, coming Fall 2013!*
Turn the page to read the first chapter of **Break Me Slowly**, Adam and Kate's book.

BREAK ME SLOWLY
CHAPTER ONE

"You need to breathe, Katelyn, otherwise you're going to pass out and I sure as hell am not hauling your ass all the way to campus myself."

I bounced in the four-inch heels, which I'd borrowed from Megan and were a half size too small. The expensive torture devices were currently cutting into my little toe.

"What do you mean, all the way to campus? It's right across the street." My order came up and I grabbed my soy latte.

"It's still too far to drag you." Megan took a sip of her coffee. Her sun-kissed skin and platinum blond hair made her look more like a beach babe than a city girl. "You just need to take a deep breath…" Megan inhaled deeply and locked her brown eyes on me, expecting me to mimic her. So I sucked a breath in through my nose and released it through my mouth. Every draft of oxygen calmed the familiar hum of anxiety pulsing through my veins.

"Good," Megan said in a soothing voice she had picked up from all those yoga videos she forced me to watch—and participate in—with her.

Despite making me exercise, she was amazing. Ever since second grade, when Bridget Burgess pushed me off the monkey bars, slinging a string of insults directed at everything from my ratty clothes to my white-trash mother and effectively throwing me into my first panic attack, Megan had stood up for me. From the age of seven, she had always been there, reminding me to breathe and trying her damnedest to keep me from the brink of a meltdown.

"You're going to be great today, Katelyn. You're one of the top students in the program and the professor is going to love you."

"Thanks, Meg."

We stepped out into the busy downtown Chicago morning. Traffic was booming. The cool September weather was crisp and carried the smells of gasoline and pastries fresh out of the oven. This time of year, when red and yellow leaves blew past the skyscrapers like tiny flecks of paint, was my favorite.

Megan held out her hand. She knew I wasn't a hugger. People coming into my personal space made me uneasy, no matter how much I trusted them. And there was no one I trusted more than Megan. But having lived for years with my mother's fists and nails coming at me, I shied away from any physical contact.

Reaching out, I took her hand. She gave it a gentle squeeze. "Remember, if anyone gives you trouble, gets too close, or you feel like you're on the brink of a panic attack—"

"I know. I need to breathe."

She nodded. "And if that doesn't work, you just give their face a high five and run."

I laughed. Megan wasn't the only person who knew about my past, but she was the only one who was aware of how it affected me.

"I'll see you tonight. Good luck!" Megan's hand slid from mine and she walked toward my uncle's real estate firm.

We had graduated last summer with our undergrad degrees. Megan now worked for my uncle, Tim St. Roy, while I'd made the choice to return to school and go for my master's in sociology. Two more years of school and volunteering at the Children's Home and I'd be on the fast track to being a full-fledged social worker.

With every step, the clicking of my pumps on concrete sent a shiver up my calves. But when my heel got momentarily stuck in a crack in the pavement, I faltered. One of these days I would have to learn to walk in these damn shoes without looking like a stumbling drunk person.

I ran a hand through my red curls, trying to tame them—not working—and continued my trek toward the university.

Graduate school had been tough to get into, but when the opportunity to T.A. for the head of the sociology department opened up, I'd jumped at the chance.

Clutching my coffee, I fished my cell phone out of my purse to check the time—

A horn blared and headlights flashed.

A shriek caught in my throat as I stared down a black town car coming straight at me. Brakes screeched, I jumped, and my coffee tumbled down the front of me.

The car stopped abruptly, just inches from my toes. Air finally found its way from my lungs as I struggled to breathe. Almost being crushed by oncoming traffic was not my ideal way to start the week. I stood dazed in the middle of the street, into which I hadn't even realized I had walked.

"Are you all right?" The driver stood by his door. He was older and outfitted in a black hat and jacket. The chauffeur.

Looking down at my ruined blouse, I slowly nodded. My knees shook as I made my way back to the sidewalk. Once I stepped up on the curb, my body relaxed a bit. The driver got into the car, pulled up alongside me, and parked.

"Miss?"

Standing outside the back passenger door was a man dressed in a three-piece, steel-gray suit and dark purple tie. His eyes were like frosted ocean water, two icebergs shinning at me.

His black hair was thick and coiffed perfectly in a rugged yet professional way that made my heart beat harder.

The driver stayed behind the wheel this time while the sinfully corporate-looking man walked toward me on the sidewalk. Those intense eyes never left my face.

"You should watch where you're going."

"I…" I looked up at him. Even in Megan's four-inch heels, he towered over me. Jesus, he had to be pushing six-three.

He was close enough that I could smell him. Crisp and clean and amazing. He radiated power and confidence, from his broad shoulders to his lean hips. Who knew suits could look so good on a man. Every stitch molded over him perfectly. His strength was very apparent even through the layers of expensive fabric.

"Are you all right?" His voice was deep, but this time, there was a slight rasp when he spoke.

"I'm fine. Thank you." A tremor slipped out and coated my voice.

"Can I offer you anything?" He looked down my body. Heat rushed over me. Shifting my weight, I tried to get a grip on my hectic heart rate. I knew I was staring—primarily at his mouth. It was thick and firm.

His gaze slid over me again. When it focused on my breasts, I inhaled sharply. Men had looked at me before, but none as blatantly as this. That heat that was pulsing? It surged so hot that my bloodstream caught fire.

I opened my mouth to say something, anything, then realized he was really looking at the soy latte splattered all over the front of me.

Damn!

"I—I've got to go. I'm late." And now I needed to find a new shirt.

Anger decided to spark just then, and irritation that this man—this sexy, sleek man—had interfered and made me feel all…weird.

Even though it was I who had walked into the street—and I who was lingering like a goon, undressing him with my eyes. Still! This morning was turning to hell quickly, and standing in the middle of downtown Chicago looking like a rumpled mess and being stared down by Mr. GQ was not helping.

"I must insist on giving you a ride."

I glared at him. Hating how cool and calm he was. Hating that he was standing there like chiseled perfection while my hair was frizzing by the second and the sugar from my coffee was sticking to my chest. A moment ago I had been keenly aware of all his earth-shattering attributes. I had never paid any man such attention before. But that was drowned out by the awareness of my own shortcomings and general lack of grace.

I was a twenty-three-year-old virgin, a fact I rarely gave thought to, but for the first time, I felt like it was written all over my face. The second dose of heat that burned through me was much different than the first.

Shame.

Embarrassment flooded me and I just wanted to get away from this moment. Adrenaline was crashing. I needed to run. From him. From this whole situation.

"I don't take rides from strangers." The Walk light was now flashing across the street.

"What is your name?"

My gaze landed back on him. "Katelyn."

"Well, Katelyn, I really must insist on giving you a ride." The way he said my name made a shiver roll across my back.

"No need, I'm just right there." I pointed to the university and moved in step with the foot traffic and crossed the street.

Careful not to look back.

● ● ●

I snatched a shirt from the campus bookstore on my way in. While it didn't go with my heels and pencil skirt, it was dry. When I walked into Professor Martin's office, he eyed me with confusion.

"Well, I admire your school spirit," he said, his belly rumbling with each word. A brown sweater vest atop a tan button-down and chocolate corduroys completed Professor Martin's look. The only contrast to his obvious obsession with earth tones was his half-bald head and white mustache. He sort of looked like Santa's second cousin.

"I've heard wonderful things about you, Miss Gunn." He gestured for me to sit. The room had rich wood furniture, like the big desk he sat behind and the matching chairs in the corner, and was decorated in different hues of chestnut. Go figure. From the carpet to the paintings—brown, brown, and more brown.

"Thank you so much. I am excited to be your assistant this year."

"Tell me, what is your long-term career goal, Miss Gunn? Academia or workforce?"

I folded my hands in my lap. "Well, I'd like to be a social worker."

He sat back and nodded. "I see. That can be difficult. Takes a tough skin to see what goes through there sometimes." He smiled. "But they need all the good people they can get."

I couldn't help but smile back. Professor Martin was nothing like what I'd expected. He was just so…jolly.

"I'm teaching a full load this term. Everything from entry-level sociology to upper division. I'll need you to hold regular office hours, and, if you think you're up for it, I would like you to step in and lecture my Soc one-oh-one classes from time to time."

"I'd be happy to, Professor."

"I've seen your transcripts—very impressive." He winked. "I think that you will do really well here."

"Thank you."

"Here's my schedule." He handed me a piece of paper with the times and days he taught the various classes. "And these—" He circled the Tuesday and Thursday evening sociology classes. "—will be the lectures you take over."

"Great! When would you like me to start?"

"Might as well start at the beginning."

"Tomorrow?"

"That work for you?"

Excitement bubbled. "Yes, of course." I was going to teach. A *real* college class. Granted, the first day was always short and generally you went over the syllabus and expectations, but it was still something!

The morning might have started out a bit rough, but things were looking up. Somewhere between a near-death experience, a sexy stranger with intense blue eyes, and Soc one-oh-one, I was feeling like my life just might be finding an even keel.

* * *

Professor Martin had left right after giving me a spare key to the office and telling me to make myself comfortable. It took only an hour to select my office hours, cross-reference Professor Martin's schedule with mine, and successfully color-code and organized every weekday in my personal planner. Right as I opened my laptop to tackle my thesis paper, a man entered the office.

"Can I help you?"

"Delivery for a Katelyn Gunn."

"That's me."

The man handed me a rectangular box wrapped in shiny white paper, with no card or any identifying writing on it. Odd.

Even though I had lived with my aunt and uncle for the last part of my high-school career, we weren't necessarily close. They had never once sent me anything. The only time I spoke with my mother was when she needed something, and I'd just seen Megan this morning. That girl couldn't keep a secret to save her life, so if she had gotten me something, I would have known then.

The messenger left and I unwrapped the mystery box. It was thin and light. When I pulled the last of the paper away, I saw the top of the box and frowned.

Saks Fifth Avenue.

I popped the lid off. Inside was a white silk blouse in my size. The card on top said:

Keep your eyes forward.
~A

What the hell?

How had he found me? Being borderline worried about the logistics of that should have been my first thought. Instead, I felt a little giddy and flattered.

A small smile tugged at my lips. Had he picked this out himself? Probably not. He looked like one of those important people who had others do things for him. He had a personal driver, for God's sake.

The color of his eyes alone was seared into my memory. That intense stare could likely burn right through a person. A man like that had power. Not just in general, but power over women. That much was obvious. It was also clear that he was very aware of his effect on others.

Before I could let the embarrassment of this morning engulf me, I switched my thoughts to something else. Like the line of his strong jaw. Judging by his dark features and careful grooming, he probably had to shave every morning and by every evening he'd have a five o'clock shadow. He had to be in his thirties, but he was fit and obviously took care of himself. So much strength and poise seeped from every pore that he could easily pull off late twenties if not for those eyes. There was darkness in them. A kind of wild knowledge that no twenty-something could pretend to have without actual experience.

My skin broke out in goose bumps and I had to shift in my seat to alleviate the sudden throbbing between my legs. What was happening to me? My experience with men was minimal. It was hard to date when I didn't like people coming within striking distance, let alone touching me intimately. My sex life consisted of myself, a few imaginary fantasies, and that was about it. But this mystery man? Just thinking of him had my whole body pulsing to life and all five of my senses begging for him.

Leaning back in the chair, I looked at the ceiling and groaned. Emotions of any kind were not fun to deal with. Which was why I tried not to. I had been on the receiving end of my mother's rage and love for years. That was the tricky part of dealing with someone who was bipolar. I never knew which version of her I'd get. She could go from such hate to such joy in a matter of hours and it wasn't until I felt her nails slice across my face that I knew which state she was in.

Even keel. All the time. That's where I preferred to be. That was where it was safe.

Now if only I could get my stupid body to understand that.

● ● ●

For more information about Joya and her books, visit www. JoyaRyan.com.

Books by Joya Ryan
The Shattered Series
Break Me Slowly (Shattered #1)
Possess Me Slowly (Shattered #2)
Capture Me Slowly (Shattered #3)–Coming Fall 2013

Made in the USA
Lexington, KY
11 July 2015